ALSO BY NANETTE L. AVERY

BLANK

BLANK

Nanette L. Avery

Blank

Printed in the United States of America

ISBN (Print): 978-1-66785-252-2
ISBN (eBook): 978-1-66785-253-9

For
Anna and Thomas
Thanks for always making me smile

Blank

War is not a single venture but rather a swarm of activities that mutate like a monstrous germ.

Prologue

One day the sun brought darkness,
grave silence, grey, ashy, and then Blank.

Positioned in the middle of the timeline is Blank. It is a space indexing the unknown for no apparent reason other than a timespan somewhere in the late 21st century perished. This is not to say that a great amount of energy was spent looking for it. Dozens of generations labored over its unfortunate demise. But after centuries and an addendum of added decades, humanity's interest in its absence ceased. People grew tired of waiting for an official explanation. Some defined Blank as the time of nothing; however, this interpretation defies the most ancient logic. To say that nothing exists excludes the fact that nothing is not empty. There are others who account for Blank as a void, the realm where things remain when they no longer exist. But here lies the problem. How did the passing from substance to void arrive? The missing piece in the timeline signifies an absence of the past, memory, and experience. Intellectually fertile yet

1

completely barren, the emptiness is represented by a ray with two endpoints. This independent and distinct interval awaits a narrative. And so, in this framed emptiness known as Blank, there are a few who are still searching for some history.

Part I

After Blank

Chapter 1

The most unsettling thing for a drunk is to wake up and ask yourself, "What the hell happened?" Still groggy, you sit up and look around. How do you explain a vacant chunk of time devoid of any existence? This happened to the world centuries ago, not the drunk part but an unexplainable hole in the virtual timeline. It was an anomaly that at first appeared as a temporary interruption. Patches of explanations were conspired, sobering most of the planet's population into a satisfied stupor. And like many unexplainable events, it slowly and inconspicuously funneled into the past and spilled over into the present as the norm. That is until recently when curious citizens of the planet began to rehash the questions of its whereabouts. The remoteness of the lost years started to follow these interested seekers like tired travelers looking for a place to rest. But, when the progression of time was determined as only moving forward, it clotted their illusions with the realization that only memory could lead them back.

* * *

They were like a pair of lone cats, walking quickly so no one would notice they had seen something they shouldn't have. The sight of the distant watchtower made them shiver even in the hot afternoon. Was it a coincidence, or had they passed the same man on another watchtower? The breeze was kicking up the dusty road, and the older sister wiped the soot from her eyes with the back of her sleeve. She stopped to listen, keeping her eyes skyward, and smiled. "If it weren't for the neighbor's dog, we never would have known she was in there," Danube exclaimed.

"Maybe that would have been better. Did you see the way she's wrapped in that old shower curtain? Good thing she found it, or else she'd have been naked!" Amazon giggled.

The gleam in Danube's eyes widened with the thought. "I bet we could get a big reward if we told someone."

"Did she see us?"

"I don't think so. It's pretty dark in there."

"Maybe she'll be gone when we get back home."

"Maybe," said the elder sister.

The man on the watchtower, a graceful-looking young person, stood at attention, rigid, with glassy eyes staring straight forward. "I don't give a rat's ass about you!" But the guard never stirred, refusing to acknowledge the mocking below. "Come on down, and we'll get into it, why don't you? Coward son of a bitch." A boy, not more than ten years old, laughed wildly as his friend continued to taunt. But still, the sentry stood stalwart.

The sisters avoided the towers for no other reason than to not attract attention to themselves. Today they had little choice; it was stationed on their most direct route. "Those two are always doing something they shouldn't," the youngest girl whispered as they crossed the road. "If they come this way, just ignore them. And whatever you do, don't mention what we found." It was hard not to look over, especially when the boys began to pelt rocks in the direction of the tower, never hitting their target but getting in a close enough range to be a nuisance.

"I think he moved!" squealed Alabama. "Did you see?"

"No, but watch this; I bet I can knock his cap off!" Nevada picked up a stone and, with an exaggerated pose, leaned back and aimed. Even the girls across the road stopped to watch. It took only a few seconds and the right amount of aerodynamics for the projectile to sail upward, only to miss its mark and strike the back of the watchman's neck. Not a sound was uttered when the head fell forward, breaking free and smashing into pieces upon impact of the cement floor.

"Shit! Run, run for your lives!" commanded Alabama.

Nearly too stunned to move, the four children heard the alarm and scattered like ants. A half-dozen dogs started to bark with shouts of disbelief expelled between yelps. Khanna removed the rifle from the wall and threw open the door leading to the top of the tower. Deputy Gris followed behind, toting a revolver in his left hand and a napkin in the other.

"That one's the last of an era," sighed Khanna as he bent over the shards of plastic. "Damn shame." Gris wiped his beard with the napkin. The crumbs scattered to the ground as a blackbird eyed the fallen pieces.

"I don't suppose there're any others?" he asked with hope tied to his question.

Khanna, a gruff man, short, stocky, but quick for his size, laughed. "What's the matter, afraid I'll put you up here instead? Don't worry. I won't waste a good man with such a menial task. Besides, you make too good a cup of coffee." He laughed and then looked down sourly. "Damn waste, damn kids. I'll put in a requisition, but it could take a month before we get an answer. These beauties were built long before our time."

"Seriously?" Gris remarked.

"Oh yeah, I'm surprised a few have lasted as long as they have." He stroked his beard and pondered his next thought aloud. "And now, I've got to report this!" A sense of dread caught in his throat as he contemplated the probable repercussions.

Gris swallowed hard and nodded. He bent over and picked up a fragment. "What's this?" He raised his palm, displaying a tiny paper-thin chip. "It must have blown out of the head when the skull shattered." He brought it up for the other man to see. "Looks like a code."

Khanna pushed it with his stubby finger. "Haven't a clue." Gris shrugged and tossed the chip back to the ground. "We better get back downstairs," Khanna said.

"I wonder if it had a name?" the Deputy asked as they threaded their way back down the narrow stairs. "It would be funny if it had a name," he laughed, "don't you think?" A half-eaten sandwich was waiting for him just as he had left it, sitting on a piece of waxed paper. He sat down at his desk and fingered the bread. "It's hard now." Gris scowled and threw the sandwich into the trash. Now he had nothing else to look forward to until supper.

* * *

Amazon wiped her eyes with the back of her hand. "You killed that man," she sniffled.

"Don't be an ass," Nevada said. "They'll just put a new head back on."

"New head, how can they put on a new head? You knocked it off. I saw it with my own eyes. It just snapped and flew off!" Amazon cried. Although alarmed, she couldn't help but be impressed by the boy's sharp aim.

"I don't see what you're all worked up about. If you're that worried, come on, and I'll show you." Alabama placed his fingers to his lips and slowly raised himself up. The irrigation ditches often provided a safe hiding place, and today was no different. He beckoned for the others to quietly follow. Amazon hesitated as her sister pulled on her sleeve. This was an adventure Danube didn't want to miss. Her young life was dull; nothing ever seemed to happen until now.

"I don't want to go," whispered Amazon. "What if we get caught?"

"Well, you can stay here, but I want to see." Life seemed to be awakening in a single morning. One waits a lifetime for murky waters to clear, and unexpectedly there was a settling.

Maybe today, she would see the bottom. Danube turned her head and gave her sister a disappointed look and then started after the two boys.

* * *

Dakar Hamlet felt as if she were sitting on the end of a tree branch, and someone was about to saw off the limb. *The North American Seed Bank* had been sabotaged. The "dry chain" mechanism protecting the integrity of several collections was severely compromised when the seed storage compartments were deliberately unsealed. The saboteurs succeeded in breaking through the facilities' barriers without leaving any traces or clues before setting off the alarm. Nothing appeared to be taken; however, so much had been stolen. The collection looked intact to the layman, but beneath the seed coats, the embryos were damaged.

The researcher sipped her Chablis and recounted the newscaster's comments. "This treachery has far-reaching consequences, but no one has described this seditious act so bluntly as Bank Director Rosario Patria, who was heard saying only four words before taking her own life. 'This is the end.'" Dakar leaned her head back, fabricating an image of the dead woman. The body contorted on the floor, a pistol resting in her right hand. Bony fingers dusted in gun powder. Death in the middle of the day seemed so senseless. Dakar wondered how the woman could have gotten a weapon. *They never said she died by gunshot.* Why had she thought that? She swallowed the last of her wine, aware of her irritation. She had spent a decade researching, identifying, and preserving native seeds. Her expertise in ethnobotany led her to the Caribbean, tracing their origin to 15 different varieties of yuca, squash, and maize. She was a potential target for agitators, none of which seemed to phase her. Her annoyance was with the Director, who had become a fatalist.

She sat motionless except for the nervous swing of her crossed leg. It would be hard to find someone to replace Patria. Trust was a difficult thing to replenish. She heard a feeble knock and turned towards the door. "Who is it?" A second more hurried rap activated her curiosity. Through the peephole, she could see a courier not more than sixteen years old, straddling his bicycle between his long legs. An envelope slipped under the door. "Just a moment!" She turned to look in her bag for a tip, but the messenger was in a hurry and sped away. It was stupid to have asked the courier to wait. If they had been seen together, she might have been able to talk her way out of the situation, but the boy, not likely. She chastised herself for having put the messenger in danger and decided to pour herself more Chablis. "How many good glasses of wine are ruined by reading a letter?" she thought and tossed it aside. She wasn't about to do that now.

Chapter 2

The potting shed needed more than a coat of paint; it needed rotten wood replaced, shingles restored, and a new door hinge. Its solitary window smudged with fingerprint letters that read, CLEAN ME. But inside, there didn't seem to be a thing wrong with it, except for a stranger.

"Where've you been? I've been sittin' on this stoop for hours!" Amazon complained when she saw her sister approaching. She stood up and brushed herself off.

"I saw the headless guy. It's not a real man."

"What do you mean, not a real man?"

"Just like I said. It's a dummy that moved. Like a mechanical man, only it looks real. And," she announced with satisfaction, "Alabama took a piece of its broken head as a souvenir. He let me bring it home to show you, but he wants it back." Danube offered her little sister the fractured piece. "Read what it says!"

"Made in occupied United States." Amazon handed it back. Her curiosity peaked, and now she wished she hadn't been such a coward.

"Cool, right?" Danube gloated and shoved the relic into her pocket. Amazon hated to admit it, but it was cool. She should have gone with her sister. Next time she'd go.

Amazon pointed to the door. "What are we going to do with the naked person. We can't leave her in there."

Danube walked over to the window and put her face up against the glass. "Don't you think it's kind of weird that nothing ever happens, and today, for no reason, two unexplained events?"

"You know what they say; things happen in twos," Amazon explained. She joined her sister at the window, but neither could see inside; the glass was too dirty.

"Who says that?"

"They."

"They?" parroted Danube back.

"Yea, they."

"Oh, those theys." It was apparent Danube understood.

"When I open the door, you go in and see if she's still there." The suggestion seemed fair to the youngest.

"Why me, you first!" ordered Danube allowing her sister to pass. "Go on; I'll be right behind you."

It was now a matter of pride, Amazon decided. She couldn't show she was scared; once was enough. She pushed open the rickety door, peered in, and stepped forward, moving gingerly around the workbench. "Helloooo?" Tiptoeing to the back of the shed, she peeked behind the mulch pile. "She's dead!" Amazon cried, jumping aside to let her sister see. "She's dead!"

But before Danube could make her evaluation, the stranger twisted her neck towards them. It was neither a woman nor a child but a youth. She was rooted in her place against the wall, with her knees bent against her chest. She picked something out from her palm and put it into her mouth.

"Don't eat those!" squealed Amazon, and forgetting her fear, tried to snatch the pumpkin seeds from her hand. But the stranger clamped her fist shut and shoved what had not spilled into her mouth. "Where'd you get those?" Amazon demanded and, kneeling, challenged the greedy imposter. The youth pointed to a jar of seeds on the table. "Damn you!" shouted Amazon, "You're a thief!"

"Get out, get out of here!" cried Danube. The youth looked startled, but rather than obeying, she pulled the shower curtain more tightly around her and rested her forehead on her knees.

The sisters observed the dirty vagabond sitting motionless as if playing possum. Several deep sighs were uttered between the folds of the plastic, but she verbalized nothing, nor did she comply with the demand. The sisters had heard rumors of strange trespassers found hiding on private property but never in their town. "Now what?" asked an exasperated Amazon. "We can't let her stay here."

"Why not?" petitioned the youth. Her voice was raspy, like a violin that hadn't been played for a long while. "Why can't I stay here?" She posed the question again, this time raising her face towards the two girls. It was a most ordinary-looking face, a crooked mouth, too long a nose for her round face, and unkempt ebony hair. It was only now that they noticed she was not naked but was wearing a mute-colored dressing gown like the ones hospital patients wore.

"We thought you were naked!" laughed Amazon.

"Naked! Why would you think that?"

Danube shrugged. "Then why are you wrapped up in the shower curtain?"

"Shower curtain?" The stranger lowered the plastic and pulled it off her legs, setting it aside. A pair of ashen legs and knobby knees were exposed. "I was cold," she admitted, knocking her slippered feet together.

"And hungry," smirked Amazon reminding the youth of her theft. "Didn't they ever teach you not to steal?"

"Or trespass," added Danube with the tone of a landlady jilted out of the rent.

The blank expression given back offered no sign of remorse. It wasn't until an orange tabby showed itself that the moment of tension broke. A faint meow came from outside and grew louder as it sauntered through the open door. It slinked past the girls and up onto the lap of the stranger, only to abruptly jump off and scamper back outside.

"I don't think Montgomery likes you," said Amazon.

"If you mean the cat, I guess not," the trespasser admitted. "Animals used to like me."

"Used to?" Danube thought this was an odd thing to say.

"Yeah, back before ...," she stopped and struck an odd kind of expression as if she was not sure what she was going to say next. So, she winced.

"Before what?" inquired Danube again. "You said animals liked you before..." Silence followed the dreaded uncertainty that gripped the youth.

"I'm not sure if I should tell you." But a distant voice in her head demanded she reconsider. *Where had she heard this voice? Today was like a shadow on the wall, ready to form a dark inky blackness where she could melt away into the night.*

"You have to tell us! If you don't, we can't help you," claimed Danube.

"How do you know I need help?" the youth asked, taking refuge in the convenience of the situation.

"Look at you!" demanded Amazon. "You're wearing a shower curtain." The absurdity of the claim made them all grin.

"I suppose it's kind of strange when you put it that way. Okay, but you have to promise that if I tell you, I can have something to eat!" Both girls nodded in agreement, crossing a finger over their hearts. "Animals liked me back before the big sleep."

"So, yesterday, animals liked you," said Danube disappointed with the answer.

"No, not yesterday!" exclaimed the youth wagging her finger at them. "You promised me something to eat if I gave you my answer. And, if you don't, I'm going to destroy all the seeds in this dirty little shed starting with that jar!" Pointing to the table, she threw off the plastic sheet and jumped up. "I swear I'll smash this to the ground!" she threatened. Her pale skin stretched tightly over her knuckles as she clasped the jar above her head.

"No!" screamed Amazon. "No!" The girls stared at the thief as if besieged by evil. Turning away, Danube ran to the front of the shed and reached behind the door. A grey film of light outlined her silhouette within the open doorway. She called for Amazon to move away and, like an assassin, turned towards her victim.

"Danube?" Amazon whispered and watched her sister and the ax. The stranger dangled the jar over her head, rocking back and forth.

"Set it down, girl, set it down, or I'll cut you like a hog." The ax swayed as Danube walked very slowly.

"I want something to eat," pleaded the hostage-taker. "Food for this jar of seeds."

"Danube?" the meek voice tried to reason with her sister.

"You first. Give it to Amazon." The ax lay heavy in her small hands. She stepped slowly with the weight of the ax head dragging along the floor.

"Why do you want to hurt me?" She lowered the jar and held it close to her chest as Danube drew nearer.

"Give it to me," said Amazon extending her hand. "It doesn't belong to you."

"But it's mine too."

"And when did it become yours?" The workbench stood between Danube and her victim. She balanced the ax between her feet. "When?"

"Before you, and you!" the stranger claimed, pointing her finger at Amazon. Visibly upset, she tucked the jar behind her back.

The day had soured. "We should have told on her," said Amazon. Danube silently agreed. "We should have told on you!" This time the statement was addressed to the stranger.

"What's your name?" Danube asked.

"Alice."

"Alice?" mocked Danube. "I have never heard of that name before."

"What's it mean?" Amazon giggled.

"What's so funny. I knew lots of girls named Alice. There's even a book, *Alice in Wonderland*. That's how popular it is." But neither Amazon nor Danube showed any sign of recognition.

"Never heard of it."

"Me neither. Have you had it long?" parroted Amazon.

"Ever since I can remember, it's always been Alice. Take my word for it." Her eyes were glued to the ax. Amazon and Danube's eyes were glued on the seeds.

"Let's make a truce," Danube said. She looked over her shoulder. It was twilight. "We gotta get back. If you put the jar on the table, we'll bring you some food."

"When?"

Danube shrugged. "Later. We'll leave it on the step outside the door. You can stay here for the night." Her voice drifted around the empty space of the shed.

Alice considered this for a moment. The jar was placed on the table. The pale hand pushed the seeds to the center. "I trust you to come back."

"Amazon, Danube!" The wiry voice was that of their mother's.

The sisters looked at each other in silence. "Shhhh," whispered the eldest. "We gotta go!" Alice crouched in the corner behind the mulch pile. She remained obediently quiet. The floor buckled under her feet, but she dared not stir. Danube shouldered the ax as she petitioned her sister to follow. Like a pair of mice, they slipped away without being detected.

Chapter 3

Uncertainty woke Alice before the sun. She wrapped the shower curtain over her shoulders and drew the plastic under her chin. She had eaten all the bread left outside for her, but now morning arrived with hunger. It was a rustic shed that bore the ages of time. A dusty lantern hung on a peg nailed into a crude shelf. Curiosity preoccupied her thoughts. All these jars, she got up and dared to take one off the shelf. It was labeled MILLET. Behind it were seventeen other jars, all MILLET. She tried to unscrew the lid, but it was sealed too tight. She placed it back on the shelf and returned to the corner. Her position was not unreasonable, nor was it reasonable. She liked it better when it was dark. If she couldn't see anything, she wasn't there. Now that it was light, she was here. She deserved no credit for that. She hoped the girls would return soon, but they wouldn't. They were out looking to share their secret.

* * *

A red hound dog addressed Amazon with a yawn. It was too old and lazy to move. Just the old man on the porch stood up. Pale light fell over him as he rose from his bench. "I suppose you're here to see my no-good grandsons," he said. He walked down and stood on the top step. He was a tall man, grey and dusty. "I don't suppose it will rain today," he said, motioning to the sky.

"My mother said it might never rain again." The old man didn't answer, so she repeated the statement. "My mother said it might never rain again."

But the old man heard nothing except noise in his head. Coughing and sneezing, wheezing, belching, some hacking, annoying involuntary human expulsions. The girl's voice broke through the eruptions, and he answered. "Damn stupid thing to say." He wasn't sure who he was answering.

"Suppose she's right?" asked Danube.

"Then that would be one hell of a mess," he said. He gestured to the door. "Don't wake up the baby."

"We won't." They slipped between the man and the railing. A strip of flypaper was hanging from a beam. "You first," whispered Amazon, and as Danube opened the screen door, she crept behind her sister. It wasn't the first time they had been to the house, but the first time inside. An unfamiliar smell of antiquity greeted them. They entered a small room. Oversized mahogany furniture and dark brocade filled the entire space. A bundled stack of firewood made a pile beside the sofa chair. At first glance, everything appeared old; at second glance, everything was old.

A carved banister led the eye to the second floor, where one of the good-for-nothing grandsons was leaning over the railing.

"Who let you in?"

"Your grandfather," Danube whispered. She stood at the bottom of the stairs waiting for Alabama to come down. But he didn't.

"Why are you whispering?"

"He said not to wake the baby."

The boy laughed. He skipped down the stairs and gestured for them to follow. On the kitchen floor was a bassinet. "Look inside; it won't bite!"

Danube kneeled and lifted back the bassinet hood. "It's a puppy, not a baby. Well, sort of a baby, a baby dog!"

"The old man's crackers," Alabama said. He tapped his forehead and grinned. "But harmless." The girls took turns petting the puppy that exchanged their affection with small whimpers. "So, now that you've seen the baby, why are you here?" He led them back into the living room and leaned against the sofa.

"Because we have something to show you!" Danube said. "And it's better than your headless man."

Amazon smiled and nodded. "And this is alive!"

Alabama sauntered over to the screen door and looked out. The old man wasn't on the porch; only the old hound was sleeping in the sun. He turned and glared at the girls. "If Nevada and me go with you and it's not a good secret, then you have to give us something for our trouble."

"Forget it," Danube snapped. "Let's go, Amazon," she said and tossed her head with disgust.

"Okay, okay, don't get in a mood. We'll meet you. We've got nothing better to do," he said, knowing it was time to get tobacco for the old man.

"When will that be?"

He glanced up at the grandfather clock. "When the big hand is on the twelve, and the little one on the ten."

"You can't tell time!" Amazon squealed.

"Sure I can; I just can't remember." Not the least bit phased by his confession, he pushed the door open. "Where?"

"Same place as yesterday, the ditch," Danube remarked and patted the boy on the back. "Oh, yeah, almost forgot, here's your broken piece of the dummy head," she said handing back the souvenir. He grinned and pocketed the find as she walked past him.

"Ten o'clock sharp," echoed Amazon, just in case he forgot. The rickety screen door squeaked as it closed behind them. The old man was in the garden. They didn't see him, but he was watching them. He was pulling the heads off the dry flowers and pocketing the seeds. He would take these seeds to Doc later, that is, unless he kept them for himself.

* * *

There they sat, the four of them, just out of earshot from the window. "She's in there," said Danube. "Amazon and I'll go in first; we don't want to spook her."

Nevada nodded. "And then what?" he asked.

"You can come inside and see for yourself."

His brow furrowed, but his eyes shone with delight. Alabama peeked through the scrubby bush with the conviction of a wolf on the hunt. "Go on!" he complained. "We don't have all day." But in fact, they did.

Danube pulled a piece of bread from her pocket. "What's that, bait?" taunted Nevada. She didn't answer his insipid question and motioned for her sister to follow. The boys watched as the girls approached the door, only to be startled by Alice coming up from behind the shed.

"I found the outhouse," she said with a scowl. "Don't you have indoor plumbing?"

"Some folks do," Danube said. "Here, this is all I could take."

Alice shoved the bread in her mouth, swallowing it almost whole. "Got any more?" She was disappointed by the shaking of the head no and slipped back inside. She cowered to the back of the shed and sat down in the corner, pulling the shower curtain up to her shoulders. The air hung damp and muggy. "Who's out there? I heard voices."

"Just a pair of boys," Amazon confessed.

"Are you letting them in?"

"I suppose," Danube said.

"What for?"

The question hadn't occurred to them until now. The door pushed open along with the sound of footsteps entering. The larger boy's shadow fell over the stranger. He stared down and then across to the sisters. His eyes roamed the small space until they fell on the shelf of seeds. "Shit!" he exclaimed.

Suddenly the sisters realized what they had inadvertently done. Alabama ignored the girl in the corner and reached across the shelf, picking up one of the jars. He turned to Danube and winked before returning the jar to the shelf. No one spoke for several moments.

"Which is the secret you wanted us to see?" asked Nevada, pointing first to the seeds and then to the stranger sitting on the floor.

"That's Alice," Danube said.

"Alice?"

"We found her," explained Amazon. The stranger looked from the boy to the girl. Nevada kneeled to get a better look.

"We caught her eating seeds."

"That is until Danube said she'd cut her with the ax if she didn't give them back."

"That would do it," grinned Alabama. "A good deterrent."

"So, now what are you going to do with Alice?"

"I'm staying." The shower curtain slid down, revealing a bony plate protruding above the back of her shoulder.

"What that?" Nevada asked, and as he reached forward, Alice shooed his hand away.

"Keep away from me." Her face hardened with reproach. "I said, I'm staying right here."

"Suit yourself," Alabama noted. "As far as I am concerned, you're just plain weird."

Danube couldn't help suddenly feeling disappointed. She was sure her finding Alice would have created some envy in her companions; however, they didn't seem to care one way or not about her secret. "Tell them," demanded Danube to Alice. "Tell them what you told us about animals."

"Animals," she explained, "used to like me before."

"Before when..." prompted Danube.

"Before I woke up."

"Which was...?"

"Which was a very long time ago."

"What the hell is she talking about?" Nevada asked.

"That's what we were hoping you could help us find out." Danube wasn't accustomed to asking for help. But these riddles needed a more cunning mind than her own.

"You'll never figure it out!" Alabama claimed. "She's from the nuthouse. Look at her clothes!" He pulled back the shower curtain and exposed the drab gown and muslin slippers. Alice shrieked and scrambled on all fours, frantic to retrieve the plastic curtain now in possession of Alabama. "Crazy girl!" he tormented, shaking the curtain just out of reach.

"Give it back to her!" demanded Danube. "She's not yours; she's ours." And with a mighty tug, she ripped it free from his taunts and draped it over the trembling stranger. "Here, Alice, here you are," Danube whispered and secured it around the thin body.

"We were just having a little fun!" complained Nevada. "You gotta admit, this is as weird as it gets."

The predicament amused them all except Alice. For the boys, it was funny; to the girls, it was an adventure, but to Alice, it was brutally serious. But this was not a playhouse, and Alice wasn't a doll. There were no instructions on what to do with her, so they all agreed they would do nothing, at least for the time being. "You stay here, Alice," Danube explained. The girl nodded and slipped back against the wall. Danube peered into dark eyes, sad and at the same time deserted. "We'll come back later."

Alice studied the foursome with curiosity. They were remarkably simple. She decided it wasn't going to be a challenge to give them an explanation but rather more of a challenge to convince. A commotion of chatter erupted outside the door after they left. She stood up and peered through the window. The four huddled together for a few minutes and then separated, walking slowly in opposite directions. Alice went back to the corner. If she were going to make any progress, she would have to rest. She folded the shower curtain into a square and lay down, resting her head on the plastic. It was cold against her cheek. There was nowhere else to place her head, so she turned over on her back and stared up at the splintered beams. She was waiting. She twisted her head and started to count the jars to pass the time. Then she counted the knots in the wood and back to the jars. When she got to sixty-one, she must have fallen asleep since she couldn't remember being awake.

* * *

"Why did you say it would never rain again?"

" 'Cause it might not." Mrs. Rivers continued to stitch the curtain's hem without looking up at her daughter. She could talk and stitch at the same time and stitch without talking and talk without stitching.

"How do you know?"

"Because that's what I was told, and now I'm reminding you." Her fingers moved elegantly across the bottom of the material.

"How come we still have an outhouse?" asked Amazon. She sat across from her mother while folding laundry. A pile of undershirts was stacked alongside the aprons. The underwear remained in the basket. Danube can fold those, Amazon decided.

The woman turned her face away from her sewing. It was the face both girls recognized. It was the same one she used when someone came in and walked across her just-washed floor. Nothing could divert that look. "You're lucky we got what we got."

That wasn't an answer, but Amazon chose not to pursue the question anymore.

Danube, however, wanted to. "Maybe we could get an inside toilet. The Bailiwick's have a toilet in the house."

A chill came over the room and touched the mother's face. "You were there?"

"Yes," admitted the youngest.

"What did I tell you about those Bailiwicks?"

"That they were not to be messed with," whispered Amazon.

"What was that? Speak up; I don't think your sister heard you!"

"That they were not to be messed with," the youngest replied.

"And?" asked the mother. But there wasn't any 'and' they could remember.

"And we don't know," piped in Danube.

The mother's train of thought shifted as Montgomery sauntered into the room. The feline circled the sewing basket just out of range from the hand reaching down to pet him. Instead, he jumped up on the sofa and sat in the middle of the clean clothes with the utmost content. "Seems to me that cat has more sense than my daughters." Danube, eager to admit she emerged a winner, smiled at her sister. But her grin was premature. "Keep away from that old coot," the woman brayed. "And those boys, they're trouble too." She was about to say something else when she stopped. She pulled the last stitch and knotted the thread. Danube resembled her mother in looks but not in temperament. Her hair was brown and eyes fair, but not as fair as her sister, who resembled their father. Mrs. Rivers cut a strand of thread from the spool before returning to her lecture. "The Bailiwicks are not like us," she warned.

"We know," said Danube. "You've told us a million times." Amazon's eyes widened. She turned to her sister and then lowered her gaze back to her chore.

"Revelation comes too late for many," admonished the woman. "But since you're both getting old enough to make your own decisions, I would be remiss if I didn't advise you. Don't you think?" The mother folded the curtain and placed it aside with the other items needing attention.

"I suppose," said Danube. "We'll be careful."

"We'll be careful," repeated Amazon.

The familiar set of promises satisfied the mother. They spent the rest of the morning on household chores, and when finished with lunch, Danube wrapped her leftover bread and butter sandwich in her napkin. They waited for Mrs. Rivers to go into the pantry before leaving the table and setting outside to feed Alice.

They hurried down the gravel path to the shed; however, the door was ajar when they arrived. "Maybe she's gone," Amazon lamented with the remorse of losing a dog. It was dark inside. They couldn't see the girl, but they could hear her stirring around.

"I'm cold," the stranger complained, huddled on the floor in a cocoon of plastic. "And I'm wet. The roof leaks." She tilted her chin towards the beams. Several large wet spots stained the rotten wood. "I opened the door to get some fresh air, but it let in the cold."

"We have some bread for you." Danube withdrew her hand from her jacket pocket, offering the miserly lunch.

"I'm not hungry," Alice said. "I'm too cold to eat."

"She needs a blanket," Amazon pointed out, "and something else to wear." Keeping this girl was becoming a chore. "Maybe we should tell on her."

"Tell who?" Danube asked. "You heard Atlanta; she said we were old enough to make our own decisions."

"Since when do you call Mother by her first name?"

Danube shrugged, "Today. Anyway," she continued, "we have to figure this out ourselves." She looked around the shed for an idea but came up short. "We'll have to borrow some seeds and go buy a few things." The suggestion was bold but necessary.

"Borrow, or do you mean steal?"

"Well, how else are we going to get what we need?" Danube challenged.

"She can have my blanket, and you can give her one of your dresses."

"We'll give her one of my dresses and buy a blanket." Danube turned to the shelf and pulled out a jar. "Sunflower seeds," she said and twisted off the lid. Amazon held her breath while her sister counted out 12 seeds and placed them into her handkerchief. "This should get us a hand-me-down blanket."

"Where?"

"Doc's." The voice was audibly low but firm enough for the younger sister to find her courage to agree. "I'll carry the seeds but, if anyone comes up to us, just don't look guilty." Amazon nodded yet fretted that she might inadvertently give away their secret. "We're gonna leave the bread here," Danube explained to Alice and placed the sandwich on the workbench. "You better eat it soon, or the mice will."

"Mice?" More wary of her surroundings, she lifted her hand from beneath the plastic and spread her palm out. "I'll eat it now." There would be time to deal with mice, but not now, even though, she thought, now was unobtainable, now never stays in one place. Once you say now, it's over. Alice smiled to herself; she would have no dealings with the mice now since now just came to an end.

The sisters had no plan. They were supposed to be looking for dried flowers before the scavengers were allowed in. But this was far more urgent. Amazon pulled the door shut behind them without looking back. She scampered beside her sister. "What if Alabama was right? What if she is from the nuthouse?"

Danube scoffed. "They don't keep kids in the nuthouse."

"Then where do they keep the crazy ones?"

"Nowhere because there aren't any crazy kids. They only become crazy when they grow up." Danube patted her bulging pocket. It was risky to be walking around with currency, even in such small denominations as sunflower seeds. She looked at her watch. "We have to hurry."

* * *

The girls crept between the wires, which long ago had formed the barrier. They set forth across a yellow-green field where the only plants that flourished were creeping thistles and nutsedge. "There it is!" exclaimed Danube. Like a relic excavated from long ago, the grand oak appeared in the near distance. "If we could find just one acorn, we'd be rich, really really rich."

"And really really in trouble if anyone were to see us here."

"I know," Danube regretted. A barbwire barrier surrounded the oak, and a posted sign warned of prosecution for anyone intruding beyond the 10-foot limit. But despite the warning, a blackbird deliberately defied the message by landing on one of the tallest boughs. The girls approached the great tree with awe. "Do you think trees can remember things?"

Amazon lifted her chin and gazed up at the canopy. The branches sagged under the cloak of leaves. "I suppose they have to; otherwise, when it comes time for them to make new buds, they wouldn't. They'd have to stand naked even after winter." She tilted her head further back and saw more than an outline against the clouds. "Why aren't there more trees like this one?"

Questions like this hurt Danube's brain. They had strayed far from the usual chatter and delved into unspoken territory. "I should've come alone," the sister scolded, diverting the attention away from the oak. "Hurry up and keep your mind on our mission."

"Alice," said Amazon.

"That's right, Alice."

The walk to Doc's wasn't far, just rustic. Not many traveled outside the restricted limits. Only a few families, many years back, managed to elude the order to resettle, but over time they were judged to be outsiders and ultimately renegades.

* * *

The yellow house stood out like a daisy in a field with just enough curiosity to lure anyone venturing by to its walkway. A woman stood on the threshold of the open door. She didn't move for a minute and then summoned the girls forward with a distrustful face. "You from town?" she asked.

"Yes. Ma'am."

"Leskov?"

The eldest nodded. "How'd you know?"

"It could only be Leskov or Shimla, and by the looks of your shoes, I would say Leskov. If you were from Shimla, your tracks would have come from the left." She gestured with her hand and smiled. "You must be thirsty," she said. "Go on back and help yourself. There's a ladle hanging from the pump."

The two girls said nothing and followed the footpath around back. The woman waited by the stoop until they returned. "That was fine water; best I ever drank," Danube explained.

"That's cause it's spring feed." The woman was holding a cloth in her hand and dabbed her brow. "So, have you come to buy or to gawk?" she asked.

"We come to buy," Amazon answered.

"Okay then, let's do some business." Doc entered the house first and led them into a parlor. The hem of her skirt dusted the floor, and as she walked, a pair of leather boots with a silver toe-box peeked out. The room had a smell, not a domestic smell, but smells of exotic scents dispensing an atmosphere of secrecy. They walked through a low-lit corridor until they came to a stairwell at the end of the hall. Humming softly to herself, she led the girls down the narrow passageway of stairs. "If you turn to the left," the woman said, "it will take you to the laundry room. We're going right," and they proceeded down to the next landing, isolated from all other surroundings. Doc reached for the wall switch and turned on the fixture, illuminating a spacious room with walls washed in blue paint where the eyes could not fix on any one spot, for it was spilling over with a hodgepodge of furnishings, knickknacks, shelves, and trunks. "You haven't told me what you are looking for."

"A blanket," Amazon said.

"For you?"

"No, for…" But as soon as Amazon spoke, Danube squeezed her arm.

"No, it's for me," the eldest girl lied.

"Aye," said the old woman. "I've got one or two here somewhere. I suggest you start with those steamer trunks." Her grey eyes fixed upon Danube as she adjusted her glasses. "Help yourself and look while I pour you each a glass of milk. It troubles me to think of you without a blanket."

"Yes, Ma'am," nodded Danube soliciting a bit of sympathy with a woeful expression.

Amazon's pale eyes sparkled as she fixed her sight on the curio cabinet. Behind the glass panes were trinkets, cups and saucers, jewelry, and mechanical toys. Her eyes roamed the deep shelves as if piercing the fog for a glimmer of light. "What's that?" She pressed her finger against the glass, pointing to a palm-size box with two small knobs and a circle of pinprick holes. But Danube ignored her sister and knelt beside a trunk. She lifted off the lid and rummaged its contents. "This is weird." An orange-colored jacket made from a sticky material much like a shower curtain was tossed aside. Other items attracted their own exclamations: a mink stole still with a pointy snout and tiny feet, a gentleman's embroidered silk robe, terrycloth bath towels, and a yellowing lace-fringed tablecloth. It wasn't until she unhinged a smaller trunk that the pungent smell of winter preparations accosted her. A bundle of blankets balled up in the bottom compartment reeked from mothballs. She lifted one out, a bit frayed yet big enough for a picnic lunch. It was the color of the morning sky after a dream you can't remember, faded blue.

Doc slipped into the room and set two glasses of milk on the table. Amazon exclaimed, eyeing the shelving as if it were a meadow of wildflowers. "Where did you get all this stuff?"

The proprietor handed a glass of milk to the girl. "From here and there, a peddler stops by, sometimes folks like you wander in to trade, and sometimes I find them." The girl appeared satisfied with the answer and thanked the woman for the milk.

"How much for this?" Danube asked, showing her the blanket.

Doc felt the corner of the material. "Genuine sheep's wool," she said, rubbing her fingers on the cloth.

"What other kind of blanket would it be?"

Doc grinned. "What's your offer?"

Danube wasn't sure what to say and pulled from her pocket the handkerchief bundle. Then she turned her back to the woman and counted out her seeds. "Here," she said, and turning forward, raised her palm. "12 sunflower seeds."

"That all you have?" the curious woman asked.

"Yes, Ma'am."

"Well then, I guess we got ourselves a deal." She plucked the seeds out of the outstretched hand and dropped them into a glass ashtray. Danube rolled up the blanket and tucked it under her arm. "Your milk is on the table." The woman cocked her head and gestured.

"You'll like it. It's cold," Amazon said to Danube. "Good and cold."

Danube raised her eyes suspiciously as she swallowed. The milk was cold, colder than she ever remembered. "We got to get home," she announced and handed the empty glass to Doc. They followed the proprietor back upstairs and through the hallway to the front door. "My name's Danube. My sister's Amazon."

"Well, Danube and Amazon, I hope your friend likes the blanket." Neither challenged the woman's claim; it didn't matter what she thought; they had what they had come for. Doc leaned against the post as the girls stepped out from under the overhang and into the sunshine and dust. "Amazon and Danube, like the rivers." But it was more than a witless observation, and as the two slowly dissolved into the mirage, she turned back inside. "They'll come back," she said aloud. "The young ones always do."

* * *

Before he knew what he was doing, Alabama had returned to the potting shed. Cruelty made you bitter inside, and he needed to right a wrong. He stood outside the door for a few minutes before offering a light knock. He thought he heard a faint remark in return. A delusion haunted him that something terrible would happen if he did not come back. "What are you waiting for? Come in," Alice said impatiently.

She was standing by the shelves when he opened the door and peered in. Barefooted and her hair brushed back, she looked not as wild, Alabama thought. Maybe even exotic. "I want to apologize." He remained in the doorframe as if too timid to enter.

"You were pretty much an ass," she replied without looking up and continued to rearrange the jars.

He had never been called an ass. "Ass?" he said.

"Yes, you know, someone who acts like an idiot." This time she turned to see his expression.

He nodded. "Anyway, I just came by to tell you that you're probably an okay person, and I'm sorry."

"So, you agree you were an ass?" she pressed. But before he answered, she laughed. "I can be an ass too; everyone can be. And if they don't admit it, then they're an ass!" She replaced the empty jar on the shelf and stepped around the table towards the door.

"How long are you going to stay in here?" he asked. He liked her smile.

"I don't know. All I know is I'm better off in here than out there. Except at night, when the moonlight carries me away. Do you like the moonlight?"

"I don't dislike it," Alabama said.

"Oh, you should try it. It can be very soothing, if only for a few moments."

Alice was different; he had never met anyone who thought as she did. "I will," he said, not sure what he would do in the moonlight. His eyes scanned the small shed, and he envisioned her sitting in the corner, wrapped in the shower curtain the day he invaded her private space. "Well, I guess I better get going. I have to gather some seeds."

"That seems to be the pastime around here," Alice said. Softly, simply, she spoke her mind with ease. Alabama was intrigued with her candor.

"I'll come back if you like. I could bring you some seeds," he said.

"Sure, that would be very nice."

He stepped back outside, but before shutting the door, he coolly waved goodbye. "See you," he said.

"See you," Alice replied. And when she lowered her hand, she was alone in the potting shed.

Chapter 4

Senior Deputy Khanna moved across the ancient cobblestones and through the open gate. Theirs wasn't the only guardhouse harassed, but it was the only one to lose a dummy guard. There had been no opportunity to tell his side of the story, to explain how the boys ran away before they could reach the tower. But in his silence, he mouthed the words in his head, "Sons of bitches," but he couldn't say it aloud. He was a subordinate. "Yes, Sir, we'll find them."

"Find them?" Deputy Gris gawked like a dog watching its master enter the office. "You think we can find them?"

"No," said Khanna, his voice tired with disappointment. "But what the hell would you have said?" He removed his cap and sat down. He yanked off his boot and massaged his heel.

"So, now what?"

"We go on, as usual, make a few inquiries." He pulled off his other boot and wriggled his toes. "Bring me some coffee."

"Then I suppose you don't want to hear about the latest break-in." He tried to bait his superior with sarcasm.

"If you mean the bank," Khanna shoved his feet into his boots and leaned back in his chair, "I got it all from the head office." Gris set the mug on the desk and poured himself a cup. "It was more than a break-in," the Deputy said, reciting what he had just heard. "The Director committed suicide. She left a note saying, 'This is the end of humankind.' The saboteurs penetrated security without leaving any clues before setting off the alarm."

"How do they know it was saboteurs and not a bunch of vandals?"

"Because the dry chain mechanism was deliberately unsealed. They wanted to make sure all the seed embryos were damaged. Besides, who would break into the bank and not rob it? It's reasonable to see why Patria was so upset." Khanna laughed to himself. The word upset was too muted for the situation.

"Patria?"

"Rosario Patria, the Director."

Gris nodded his grizzled head. Now that the woman had a name, she became a victim. "But why write *this is the end of humankind*? Don't you think that's a bit dramatic considering the circumstance?"

Khanna shrugged. "Who the hell knows why those fanatics say the shit they do. Probably because she found out her entire life's work was ruined."

"And the frontier?"

"What about it?"

"Do you think this break-in had anything to do with the dissidents?"

"Don't be naïve, Gris. It has everything to do with that. But are you in the mood to be a hero? Not me. I don't give a shit about the frontier or dissidents or rumors of how or why. All we gotta do is try and find those brats. Those are our only orders. So forget about the bank, the suicide, and anything else that might enter your thick skull." He set his empty cup down and smiled. "Where's the list of usual suspects? We can start with those delinquents."

Gris retrieved a folder from the file cabinet and dropped it on the desk. He sat down and pursued the list. "Petty larceny, truancy, fighting in public, underage gambling, and..." he stopped and looked up with his finger still on a name, "weapons violation."

Khanna shifted forward, "What kind of a weapon?"

"Doesn't say."

"What do you mean it doesn't say? Give me that!" His stubby hands flew across the desk. He grabbed the folder and lowered his face to the paper. "Virginia Burg, age eleven, held on a weapons violation. Found not guilty due to lack of sufficient evidence." He peered over the folder and set it down on the desk. He turned the page and continued to read. "Here's one, Alabama Bailiwick sentenced ten days in the juvenile stockade for..." he glanced up and, raising an eyebrow, offered the good news, "destruction of government property."

"Yes! Sometimes things do work out in our favor," Gris laughed.

"Even better, he lives in our district. No crossing jurisdictions. This one's ours and ours alone." Khanna handed the folder to Gris with instructions to fill out the appropriate paperwork. Then he stretched and sighed like a Labrador. "When you're done, meet me in the tower; we need to collect the remains of our broken friend. And don't forget an empty evidence box; I want'a retrieve everything."

* * *

Out of the crucible, this emotionally charged surrender by the country shaped the next generations' lives. The process of acculturation and conformity had profound effects on the invaded population, losing sight of life before the incursion. On the level of international relations, the United States, the strongest country before the great solar catastrophe, was reduced to a state of near-complete subjection.

* * *

The old man sprinkled the chervil seeds into a bag. They weren't worth much alone, but he figured he could make a decent trade together with the oregano seeds. He didn't mind collecting like some folks. For him, it was a challenge more than work. Knowing where the best fields remained was like knowing the best fishing hole. Sometimes it took weeks of wandering, and then, in an effort not to exploit the limit, you had to be very careful, lest the authorities think you are hoarding. But Trenton Bailiwick was a shrewd man and never got caught.

The shadows were nearly blue where he walked, in bedroom slippers, along the garden path back to the house. He was forgetful at times, and today he wasn't sure where he left his shoes. But it mattered not, at least not to him, what he was wearing on his feet. He sat down under the overhang and fanned himself with his handkerchief. "I wonder where that good-for-nothing boy is?" he asked the hound. But the dog was too tired to answer. Last night he seemed to roll around in bed; it was too hot to sleep or dream. So, he just lay in bed and thought. Without a dream, he just couldn't get a restful sleep. And thinking wasn't the same. Dreaming made everything better and brighter. The old man listened to the wind and wondered why he was so hot. It had been a broken-up night. His mind drifted and tore away small colorful pieces of thought.

It was nearly 6:00 when the old man rose accompanied by the same unfailing recollections he sensed every morning, a befuddled memory, which would take shape with the sun. *"Why did we leave?" he asked.*

He held his grandmother's hand so she wouldn't topple over since she was very old. Too old to be standing. "Because the whole damn place sank." Her voice was anything but frail.

"Why did it sink?" Although no bigger than she was, he helped her to the rocker.

"Because that's what happens when you don't take care of your house!"

It wasn't much of an answer when you're five. But now he knew what she meant. He craved to forget all misery and wiped his neck with the handkerchief. He saw the boy walking up the path to the house. "Where ya been?" he asked. But the boy didn't answer and offered him the tobacco. "Did you feed the baby?" he asked. The boy nodded, yes. The old hound lifted its brow as if to say, "thanks."

Alabama sat down on the step with his back to his grandfather. "How come no one ever comes by?" He twisted his head around to see if the old man was looking at him. But he wasn't. He was staring straight ahead.

"Because there are two kinds of people. Those who do and those who don't do."

"And what are we?"

"Doers. You come from a long line of sons-of-bitches, but all doers." The old man wiped his neck with his handkerchief. "I hope you don't spend your time thinking' about that kind of shit, because it won't help. You are who you are, just like I learned, and my grandfather before mine learned, and so on and so on, you are who you are."

The boy rested his elbows on his knees. "I never told you, but I think you're the bravest man I ever knew."

The grandfather cleared his throat, something he did when he wasn't sure what to say. "That's very nice of you, Alabama. Right now, you're my favorite good-for-nothin' grandson."

The boy lifted his head and laughed. He reached inside his pocket and pulled out a shard blown free from the dummy's head. He wanted to show it to the man, but he decided to wait. "What would happen if someone saw something that might be trouble?" A touch of silence followed his question. It was almost paralyzing to have said such a thing. Everything was moving at such a nice slow rate, and now he had unleashed a bomb.

"Depends on what it was that you saw."

"I didn't say I did," Alabama exclaimed. He had now turned full-face towards the old man. "It was just a what if someone saw kind of question."

"I heard you the first time," said the man. "And like I said before, it depends on what you saw." He stopped rocking and sighed. "What did you see?"

"I think I met up with the past," Alabama whispered.

The old man leaned forward. The smell of tobacco was so strong that it almost made the boy cough. "And your good-for-nothing, brother? Did he see it too?"

"Yes," whispered the boy.

"Did you let it speak?" said the old man. "You have to be careful; it can manipulate."

Against the sky, the clouds were always changing. They split into two directions. One blocked the sun and made a bit of shade; it was the closest thing to sitting under a tree. The other cloud loitered aimlessly, caring little for either the man or the boy or the hound.

* * *

The stranger said she didn't mind waiting in the garden shed. "But you can't stay here forever," Danube insisted. "Besides, won't anyone come looking for you?" Alice sat on the stool, barefooted with the shower curtain draped around her. She wasn't interested in the dress or the blanket the girls set on the bench. She looked at the bundle as if they had handed her a plate of liver.

"I appreciate your help, but I'm perfectly fine." Danube and Amazon hadn't planned on this. She was a risk, but they would never find anything like her again. "Everything I need is here. If I want to sleep, I can just curl up in the corner to almost nothing." She pulled the blanket towards her and smiled. The blanket felt soft against her skin, and she was feeling more like she could trust these girls. She unfolded the dress that was just at her reach, a pale green and lavender shift with long sleeves. "You want me to wear this?" she asked, bemused. Then slipping off the stool, she held it up in front of her and bent over to look.

"What's the matter with it?" Danube asked. It was one of her favorites. As far as she was concerned, Alice was pretty lucky. "If you want to walk around in your nightclothes, go ahead. But you'll look ridiculous when you go out."

"Go out!" She held the dress against her body and clutched it tightly. "Where to?" she demanded.

"To...?" Danube didn't know what to answer. Telling her to leave would be like letting a stray puppy loose.

"Back to where you came from," Amazon chimed in.

"I can't; that's impossible!" Alice whimpered. "I've spent a long time straddling the perimeter, except for the time since my arrival. Excuse my saying so," she professed, "but this is turning into a horrible day! Inside is hunger and thirst and smelling like dirt; outside is hunger and thirst and smelling like dirt. What's different? Nothing. And if nothing is different, they must be the same. But if the inside and outside are the same, at this rate, there will be nothing, except the same, that is different, and I've ended up back the beginning or at the front of the end." She started to whimper again.

"Now we've done it," Danube thought aloud. "Don't cry, Alice. Here, we'll leave, and you can lie down and take a nap. We'll come back in a little while with something for you to eat."

Alice nodded, tossing the shower curtain aside, and pulled the blanket around her. But she wasn't hungry; she had already eaten. She hid the jar of pumpkin seeds behind the others out of sight and wondered what would happen if they knew what she had done. There were so many things about these strange girls she didn't understand, like how anyone would wear such a silly-looking dress.

* * *

A little black spot appeared in the distance, disappearing into a white circle, and then reappearing again. "What's that?" Amazon asked.

"A bird."

"Are you sure?"

"Yes, pretty sure."

"When I sit here in the coolness of the shade, I sometimes forget what we are supposed to do."

"We're making a list," Danube reminded her. The parchment was folded in half and almost filled from top to bottom. The food necessary to maintain Alice was a problem. The sisters went over the schedule several times before coming up with the final list. Every morning but Monday, and every noontime except Wednesday, and every suppertime except Friday. Sunday at 4 in the afternoon and every other week at 3 in the afternoon. "What do you think?" Danube asked after reading it aloud. Amazon thought for a few moments and sourly handed her back a frown. "What's wrong with it?" Danube demanded.

"Well, to start, Monday morning without breakfast. That means from Sunday suppertime to Monday lunch; she'll be without food. That might be too long a stretch."

Danube crossed out the Monday, agreeing to Monday breakfast and Thursday no lunch. "We have to skip a few meals so that Atlanta won't get suspicious."

Amazon lifted the paper from the table and reread it. "Monday breakfast, no lunch on Wednesday or Thursday, and no supper on Friday. A snack on Sunday, at four in the afternoon, and every other week at three in the afternoon." She looked up. "We didn't decide which day every other week at three would fall on."

"What day do you want?" Danube asked.

"How about Saturday? That will make up for no supper on Friday."

"I can live with that," Danube agreed and wrote it down. "What kind of mid-afternoon food?"

"Bread and butter, or peanut butter on bread," Amazon said.

"That's more like lunch. Let's make it a cookie or cracker; they're more of a mid-afternoon snack."

"I suppose." Amazon agreed reluctantly. "But what if where she comes from a place where they don't eat cookies or crackers. Then what?"

"Then, she'll be hungry and can feed the mice!"

The day was bordering on unimaginative. "What do you want to do?" Amazon asked.

"To do?"

"Yes, what do you want to do?" Unsettledness gnawed at her brain as Amazon tried to get her sister to decide.

"I'd like to go back to Doc's."

"No, really, what should we do."

"You asked." Danube laughed, but then seeing it wasn't really that funny, she moved closer to her sister. "What do you say? We can borrow some seeds and go buy something, something for Alice."

The fragility of the idea lay heavy on Amazon, and the more it pushed down, it slowly began to fracture, splintering into a thousand *what-ifs*. She knew it would not be easy to put the pieces back together, so she had to agree, or else it would be swept away in doubt. She was sorry she asked, and now the only thing she could do was smile and hope her sister would forget. That was not possible, though; Danube never forgets.

Chapter 5

A renewed interest in the arts accompanied the political and cultural turmoil following the overthrow. Artists assumed satirists' roles by portraying government officials with anatomical abnormalities, grotesque caricatures, and pornographic burlesque. Such lampooning of those occupying the country delighted art critiques and the public alike. The most revered oil painting, *A Sophisticated Pig,* was reproduced so often that anyone could buy pirated prints on the black market. But before the original painting and its copies were confiscated, the fierce desire by art patrons to become socially emboldened rose in popularity. An exhibit of contemporary work, *Odessa meets Salem,* opened at the old MOMA in what was once Manhattan. The show's vulgarity was greeted with enthusiasm, delivering a clamor for another exhibit. Several months following, an even more ambitious underground project set an opening date; yet, for reasons that remain obscure, the unorthodox artists and their artwork were mysteriously unaccounted for just days before the first installation.

* * *

On the porch, the old man made polite yammering while Gris waited for the boy. "Want some coffee?" He thought he heard the Deputy answer, but he wasn't sure. "Tell me again about the weather?" The Deputy walked around the rotted plank and the old hound to the chair. "Hot," he replied.

"I told that good-for-nothin' grandson to come back soon." The white sky unwound a mirage lifting off the road. "He's got a tendency towards vagrancy," said the old man.

"I was the same way," said Gris. "I'd save up a whole week just to go to the lake to sift the muck for peasant food."

"Peasant food?" the old man rubbed his chin.

"Crab, shrimp, clams, bottom feeders," he explained.

"We call that fisherman food, that is, when it used to rain."

"Rain?" the Deputy looked up and squinted. He wiped his face with his handkerchief. "Doesn't seem to mind the dog."

"What doesn't mind him?"

"The heat." Gris pointed to the red hound sleeping in the sun.

"It does, but he just doesn't complain. It wouldn't do any good if he complained. That's the difference between him and us."

"What's that?" Gris asked.

"He never complains."

Gris couldn't help but agree. He envied the old hound: wordless, no desires, and patience, plenty of patience.

"Tell me again why you're here."

"Some trouble at the gate tower, government property was vandalized." Gris leaned back and sighed. He put his face up to the sun, a sign of resignation.

"I was wondering what we were waiting for," said the old man. "The boy, he likes to climb. Before he could walk, he would climb."

"They all do," said Gris. "Walls, fences." He stopped to think of other things.

"Rocks," added the old man.

"Rocks?"

The grandfather had a faraway look. "Yep, rocks too."

Gris felt displaced on the porch, with the old man, sitting in the sun that the dog didn't mind. But he minded and wondered if the old man minded sitting in the sun but decided if he did, he wouldn't be on the porch. Gris hated the porch. He stood up and stretched. "When Alabama gets back, tell him to come and see us."

"I thought you were here to see Nebraska," said the old man.

Gris pulled the orders from his shirt pocket and unfolded it. "No, it's Alabama. Says here, Alabama Bailiwick. I don't suppose he's inside."

"No."

"No what?"

"No, he's not inside. Just the baby."

His expression reflected his mood. Gris folded the paper and stuck it back into his shirt pocket. "As soon as Nevada gets back, tell him we need to see him."

"You mean Alabama," the old man said.

"Alabama." Gris nodded and tried to smile, but a film of dust on his lips stuck them together, so he grinned. The old man remained sitting, as did the dog when Gris stepped away. It seemed to Gris that he had been waiting on the porch for a long time. If he hadn't gotten up, he might have been there all day and all night. The man and the dog didn't have anything else to do. For him, there was little satisfaction sitting and wondering when the boy would come home. He was glad he got up and left. The burden was now on the boy. But when Alabama returned, he did not go to see Gris or Khanna. If they wanted him, they would have to find him. That's what the old man said, and he agreed not to go. It was at this time that Alabama was transferred to another place.

* * *

Dakar Hamlet finally tore open the envelope and slipped the note free. "It's Time." Dull, unsentimental, however necessary, considering what was at stake, these were the words typed, the ones she expected. She folded the note and creased the paper as she thought. It never occurred to her that her Uncle Gibraltar would not live forever, not that he was supposed to, but it was too soon for him to die; it's always too soon. She was sad, not that he was dead but for being selfish, thinking of herself at a time like this. Refusal to execute the plan was not an option. She was to expect a follow-up letter with instructions, but she would have to wait until then. It had taken years for her Uncle to amass the information compared to how little time it took him to relate it to her. "Isn't that always the way," she thought. His mustache hung over his lip like a brown caterpillar, and when he spoke, it moved. "Now, do you understand?" She nodded, yes. But the information was disjointed, patchy, crooked, even deformed. Her mother's brother, her father's brother-in-law, her grandmother's son, her aunt's husband, her cousin's father, they all were Gibraltar's, but she wasn't. She was a Hamlet, yet he chose her to inherit the past. There was one critical flaw, though, who would believe her?

She took it in her head to no longer think of her mission in one parcel but to invert the information into piecemeals of sentences and then words. Pick out the verbs first, but eliminate the past tense; that would be counterproductive. Filter proper nouns and then regular nouns; toss out adjectives and adverbs; they're like junk food. It wouldn't be too difficult to distill.

Part II

Before Blank

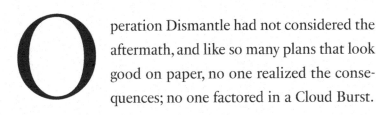Operation Dismantle had not considered the aftermath, and like so many plans that look good on paper, no one realized the consequences; no one factored in a Cloud Burst.

Chapter 6

The writer leaned back in his chair but never put his pen down. It was obvious that he was in deep contemplation, but after a momentary lapse in time, he resumed his work. He turned with a start as the girl approached. "What are you doing?" the child asked. She sat down beside the desk.

The man pulled another piece of paper in front of him and continued to write. "There," he replied after scrawling his signature. "I am finished." He appeared more than content, happy, almost boastful.

"What are you doing?" she asked. Her curiosity channeled the archaic implements her father had set before him.

"I haven't used a pen in so long that my fingers barely remember how to hold the darn thing. And this paper, it's older than you!" The parchment, monogrammed with ornamental initials, emitted a musty odor having been stored for decades in the desk drawer.

"I remember, they belonged to your great grandmother."

"Her grandmother's," he corrected. "The paper is so old that its color has turned from white to straw." The young girl turned her nose up at the musty smell.

"What did you write?"

"Ah, you want to know too?" he laughed. "The whole world will want to know." He glanced above her head and looked through the window into a fading sunset. "How would you like to take a trip to the moon?" he asked.

The child grinned. "Honestly, Father, you can be so silly." Suddenly she grew quite still; for just that second, his expression became strangely earnest. "Seriously, what are you writing about?"

"Can you keep a secret?" he asked. She nodded, yes. "Well, if you must know, it's about Operation Dismantle."

The pleasant little room they were in began to grow incredibly small. The door and the two windows drew together with only a sliver of space between the sides. The walls converged, pinching the corners of the room towards the center so curiously that the child hoped she would be able to move around. She hated when she felt confined. "Can I read it?" she asked, trying to raise her arm, but the desk had pushed towards her chair, offering little room to spare.

"Breathe," said the man. Except for the corners of his mouth, his face had squeezed so tightly that it was difficult to understand what he said. A slow, deliberate sound crept out of her nose, and slowly, the room began to stretch. "Better?"

"Thank you, Father. Now may I read it?" He handed her the papers: *Operation Dismantle.*

"Certainly, and then I will place it in the canister. Do you remember where it will be buried?"

"Ten meters from the entrance."

"It will look different when we wake up," he said. "Might be overgrown or might be barren."

She tapped her head and nodded. "I know, Father. I can't forget."

"And what will you follow if you ever get lost?"

She meditated on his words and perceived that he might not believe she would remember. One does not forget things from their first house: rooms, furniture, windows, and even toys. There would be no disorientation. All of it was formative, and so was this information. "The mole."

"That's right, the mole."

The father seated at the desk was not in charge. As one might imagine, there remained numerous thinkers, all of which used fictitious names for reasons of secrecy. Arbor carefully rolled the papers into the shape of a tube. Before laying it in the cylinder, he dropped a small chip to the bottom. There wasn't any guarantee that the cylinder would ever be discovered, but his conscience would not allow him not to try. It was self-destructive to try and subvert the plan, but at least this might help enlighten the generations after him.

* * *

"What we're proposing to do is anarchy."

His grizzly face grew into a smile. "I am not sure it is anarchy if more than one nation is involved."

"Okay, then, we'll say global sedition."

"That's probably more accurate," he agreed. "But you've been part of it all along. Why now? Why the cold feet."

The mother, who called herself Artemis, sighed. "It's just that when it happens, it's going to be a real shock." Her voice grew anxious with the statement.

"And isn't that what needs to happen? A shock, no, more than a shock, an epiphany."

She grinned. "An epiphany sounds so gentle, more like we're going to give humanity a light peck on the cheek instead of a crack across the skull." But in that grin, she released an under-standing Arbor could read; his wife was on board. If it hadn't been for her aptitude, evaluating calculation programs aligned to geomagnetic disruptions would have been delegated to the European team. "No, I know you're right. It's Alice I'm worried about. I'm not sure if the plan is worth it." Artemis poured her husband a cup of coffee and sat down across from him at the dining table. She pushed the sugar bowl in his direction. "I know what you're going to say, a hell of a time to back out." Arbor dropped his spoon into his cup and began to stir. "You didn't put in any sugar," she said.

He nodded and set the spoon on the table. "It's happen-ing with or without us. If we back out, then someone else will take our roles. Look Artemis; we have no choice." His voice was deliberately soft, but he needed to reestablish the gravity of their situation without wavering. "Let's be blunt; if nothing is done, then the planet will be irrevocably damaged. As it is, we're late, generations late."

"And Alice?"

"When she wakes up, she'll be okay."

"Tell me again why we need to go through with it now?"

"For one thing, timing. Your team came up with the results and ..."

Artemis looked up at the ceiling woefully, shaking her head. "I know, I know. The solar activity."

Arbor stood up and walked over to the window. His hazel eyes looked outside as the new day was just breaking through a bank of clouds. "Remember what happened in '59." He cleared his throat. He turned around and stared at her.

"Are you talking about that ancient history? The Carrington Event back in the 1800s. Heavens, Arbor."

"No, really, hear me out. Telegraph wires shorted out, operators were shocked, all because of solar flares."

"I know all this; the coronal mass ejections triggered a global geomagnetic disruption. Please get to the point."

"The point is we don't want to squander the moment. You do realize that this one is going to be...," but before he could complete his thought, he was interrupted by his wife.

"Catastrophic?"

"No," he said, "I was going to say essential."

* * *

Docteur Manette is not a medical doctor but rather a doctor of botany, and his partner, Sophie Germain, a bacteriologist. They emigrated from France to the Netherlands, where they were recruited to join Operation Dismantle. And, like their counterparts, Arbor and Artemis, they too use fictitious names for the same reason. Their support for the great plan was inspired by Sophie's paternal lineage dating back to the Enlightenment. On her father's side, her Uncle Joseph Martin was a master gardener, dispatched by the French government to collect indigenous plant species while navigating through the Caribbean and Madagascar. However, before his return, he had enough ingenuity to set some of the collected seeds aside for himself. If this decision were for propagation, income, or environmental foresight, his rationale remained a secret. Years later, what became public knowledge was establishing the Germain family seed bank where heritage seeds, originating from Uncle Martin's collection, remain concealed with other varieties collected.

The bench Manette and Sophie were sitting on stood low and rickety. The Docteur rested his neck against the backboard and wondered why he was so uncomfortable. He stretched his arms, almost hitting Mademoiselle Sophie with his elbow, and then stretched upward. "You're like a clumsy chien," she complained and scowled.

"Pardon, Sophie. You know how I hate to wait." The woman only scowled again and sat patiently with her hands folded on her lap. "Perhaps he got held up; then we'd be sitting here as if waiting for a plane. That's something I hate," he added, drifting off on a tangent. "Airports."

"Oui," she agreed. "I, too, hate them."

"Hate what?" Manette asked.

"Planes."

"Oh, I don't hate planes; it's airports I detest."

"That too," she sighed. "Do you have your card with you?" she asked.

"I never carry it; you know that." She sighed again and refolded her hands. "Why? Do you want something?" he asked.

"I thought I could buy us a coffee while we wait." She smiled and looked longingly at the café across the street.

"It won't be long; Elijah is never very tardy. Except now," the docteur complained.

"We should have chosen a different place to meet," Sophie said. She looked to her left. "There is not enough room for the three of us." Manette nodded in agreement. She was correct. It would be a very tight squeeze. "Do you think he likes what he does?" she wondered aloud.

"Who?"

"Ateka."

"Ateka?"

"Yes, Elijah, isn't that who we're waiting for."

"I never call him Ateka, only Elijah. Elijah Ateka."

The conversation was beginning to bore them both, so they decided just to sit quietly. Sophie wished she had a coffee, and Manette wondered what was keeping the contact.

A tall man with a black cap exited the café. A sizeable beige dog with a navy-blue sweater wagged its tail. The man bent over and held his hand out, offering the dog a sweet pepernoot. Then he stood up and waved to the couple across the street. "He's at the café," Mademoiselle said. She smiled and gestured back with an indifferent wave of her palm.

The dog and man crossed the street. The dog sat down next to Manette and sniffed his foot. "I hope you liked your pepernoot," Manette said to the dog.

"This is Inja," exclaimed the virologist introducing the dog.

"Shall we walk?" Sophie asked, standing up. "I'm sure Inja won't mind."

"We can follow her to the park; she knows the way," Mr. Ateka suggested. "I had a bit of a time getting here. I had to take a different route than usual." Docteur Manette nodded with understanding.

"Do you miss being away from your home?" Sophie asked. "I sometimes miss France," she confessed.

"I'll be back in a few days." The contact walked with a quick and determined gate. He wasn't one to chit-chat, and now was no time to change his manner. "Here," he said, reaching into his pocket. He handed both Sophie and Manette an ear nub. "It will give you the exact coordinate and date."

"The meeting tonight, Monsieur Ateka, I understand it is the final one," Sophia said, signaling her confirmation. The park was a small patch of green oasis within a concrete metropolis. Inja ran as if looking for something left behind. The grass felt soft beneath the dog, and Sophia stopped to take off her shoes. She turned to Ateka and dug her bare feet into the ground. "It will be the last of our meetings, non?" she reiterated.

"Oui, and then the fun will begin."

Manette walked towards the dog. He picked up a stick and tossed it. Inja watched as the object went airborne and fell several meters away. But instead of chasing it, as anticipated, the dog ignored the docteur's playful act. "I guess she's not amused," he called back to Elijah.

"Inja is more of a rescuer than a chaser," he said.

The three stood in the shade of the building towering outside the fenced greenspace while they watched the dog amuse itself, darting this way and that. Now that Manette and Sophie were issued their nubs, there was no reason to remain. But knowing they would likely never be together again, a slight feeling of remorse roused Ateka. He had volunteered his expertise with Operation Dismantle to secure permanent change on Earth. Experiencing firsthand the increased frequency and intensity of extreme weather events, he and those in the Southern Hemisphere lived in crisis: water, food, and energy insecurity. For decades, the region experienced an upsurge of vector-borne diseases (malaria and dengue fever), including water and food-borne diseases (cholera and diarrhea). Generations before him had good intentions; however, good intentions resulted only as a pause in the global upheaval. Humanitarian programs proved as effective as placing sandbags on the shore to prevent a tidal wave. It was evident more permanent measures needed to be taken.

"Inja!" The dog immediately responded and ran back to the voice that called her and sat by her master's feet. "I have to go," Elijah said, petting the dog on the head. "I bid you both good luck."

"Yes, luck, well, hopefully, we won't have to depend on that," Manette exclaimed.

"If all calculations are correct," Sophie chimed in, "we have nothing to worry about."

Elijah looked from the dog to Manette, to the dog, back to Manette, and then to Sophie. He reached behind and pulled from his pocket a lead and clipped it to the collar. "Take Inja with you; I won't be able to travel back home with her. Anyway, she's accustomed to life here."

"You want us to keep your dog?" Manette was taken aback by the oddness of the gesture.

"Yes. Besides, you'll need her."

"He's right, you know," Sophie agreed. "She's trained."

"How do you know?" Manette declared.

"Because Ateka mentioned it before; she's more of a rescuer than a chaser." Sophie smiled, knowing she was correct. "Does she always wear the sweater?" the new owner asked.

"Only if it is cool outside."

Sophie stroked the dog's head, and it grinned back. "Bon chance, Monsieur Ateka, and thank you for the gift." The dog wagged its tail with a satisfied impatience as it proceeded to tug at the lead. The woman obliged her new friend and started away towards the street. "Meet you back at the apartment!"

"She likes cookies, but not too many!" called Elijah. "She can be very convincing, you know!" But neither Sophie nor the companion turned back to acknowledge he had been heard.

"I'll tell her," explained the docteur stretching out his hand. "Well, this is it."

Elijah shook Manette's hand. "Whatever happens, there is no turning back. The decision to go forward is to go backward." The omission of the future was akin to taking a walk backward.

The sunlight fell over the two men, and it claimed both their attention. Whether out of laziness or nostalgia, they were in no hurry and lingered for a few more minutes. The docteur spoke first. "Have you ever read anything written on paper? I recall my grandfather owning a paper book, but it was sold to pay his medical bills. I never read it since it was kept in a locked safe."

Elijah gestured, a sign of understanding. "Paper books are so obsolete in my country that the concept of reading printed material is only cited in context to historical reference. And forget about finding paper," he mused. "With trees so scarce, to venture such an undertaking would be immoral. There was an exhibition at the university I attended; it must have been over twenty years ago. A half-dozen books were displayed in glass boxes, but it was difficult to get close enough to read the print. Even if they were accessible most of the pages had faded."

"I'm afraid everything I read is on a screen or in my ear. Not that I mind," Manette pointed out.

"I think it would be rather bohemian to go back to reading books since I am more of a Renaissance person than a conformist."

"As are most of us involved with the grand plan," challenged the docteur. "My concern lies with those in the lower decks. Then again, Sophie would say I'm an intellectual snob." Manette signed, deeply soliciting a response. A cloud darkened the ground and formed a shadow over the men.

"I wouldn't worry much about those who may or may not grasp the science behind our methodology. Some have political reasons for their responsibility towards the plan. Frankly, I don't give a damn what the reason is, which makes it easier."

"Easier for what?"

"Just easier." A man and woman passed by as they were talking. The man tipped his hat and walked briskly past with the woman, who seemed to drag one foot and limp behind. When they got to the corner, the traffic stopped and allowed them to proceed across. "A most ordinary couple," remarked Ateka. "And to think their lives will be severely interrupted in just one day."

Chapter 7

Before the great plan's blitz, all societies were globally and virtually connected; information was accessible, paperless, and immediate. All documents and reading material, past and present, were archived in digital form and retrieved through wireless transmission. Digital, cyber, and electronic currency replaced legal tender. A sense of security and power made humankind feel that they had unlimited access to knowledge. But in fact, all inhabitants had become vulnerable, exposed, and deprived of personal protection and guidance. Unaware of the changes before them, what once was, would soon be not.

* * *

"*The saboteur should never attack targets beyond his or her capacity or the capacity of his or her instruments.*" Artemis read aloud so her husband could hear. She looked at him and winked. "*The saboteur should be encouraged to attack transportation facilities of all kinds. Communication also should become targets for the citizen-saboteur.* And to think this all began with a get-together of a few minds over wine. And here we are, on a global mission to set right the mistakes of humanity." The mother pushed her screen aside and sat back in the chair.

"And consequently, abusing the planet needs to be rectified." Arbor was tired and wanted no part of the tactical review meeting. But he couldn't complain; at least he wasn't on a continent where the meeting was in the middle of the night. The timepiece showed two minutes to go. "Are you comfortable, Artemis? I could bring over the ottoman."

Artemis shook her head; everything was fine. She closed her eyes and adjusted the volume on her nubs. Arbor settled into his armchair and leaned his shoulder against the cushioned back. He fiddled with his earpiece, and then with a raise of his hand, he gestured a sarcastic goodbye to his wife.

A woman's voice belonging to Jane Eyre began her remarks. "Before we embark on the most dramatic disruption to society ever demonstrated by a coordinated event, I want to commend all of you on your collaborative determination to see this plan to the end. Our generation and multitudes of generations before witnessed upheaval and devastation to our planet. Climate change, pollution, water shortages, weakened magnetic fields, and ozone corrosion could have been averted if protective measures had been initiated at the onset. But, due to negligence and indifference over centuries, we are brought together at our most decisive moment. In only ten hours, committed allies of Operation Dismantle from every hemisphere on the planet will dramatically change life on Earth." Arbor shifted restlessly in his chair as he listened. He sensed an urgency in Eyre's tone that he hadn't noted before. "Our coordinated efforts will likely be misconstrued, unfairly judged, and universally condemned. But positive notoriety is not the objective. The objective is to render all communication useless." He was feeling hungry. He had eaten a chicken salad sandwich not too long ago, but his stomach must have forgotten that and persisted in reminding him of his appetite with grumbling noises. "In ten hours, solar storm #235 will emit coronal mass ejections as it proceeds on a direct trajectory towards Earth. The stripping away of our planet's protective magnetosphere will last approximately 8 hours, setting in motion the absorption and disruption of high-frequency radio transmissions, universal power systems, and infrastructure failures, devastation to satellite navigation systems, and aviation transmission. Universal methods of communication, ground and rail transportation, and all commerce, will collapse. If executed according to our projection, our simultaneous sabotaging of all power grids during this event will trigger cataclysmic disruptions to worldwide communication, associated technologies, and the global economy. Crippling power failures, as I have described, and you have engineered will dominate the planet."

Artemis opened her eyes and blinked. She sat forward as she listened to a list of instructions, none for her. She had satisfied her part of the initial preparations, calculating the exact course and timing of solar storm #235. The opportunity for another geomagnetic storm of this scale within the next decade was only 12%. For the first time in a long time, Artemis realized the genius of the plan. She wondered if Arbor was still listening or if he had tuned out. An hour had passed since the beginning of the review meeting. They were obliged to attend, but fewer words would have been sufficient. A chill fell over the room, and she pulled the afghan from the floor over her legs. "For the whole world and especially for the saving of our planet, I bid you all good luck." The voice was soft, almost angelic. Artemis looked over at Arbor, who appeared to be asleep. Funny how peaceful he looks. She pulled the nubs from her ears and set them on the side table. There were no directives on what to do afterward. She and Arbor had made plans; as for the others, she didn't know. At any other time, this would be wrong. But not today. In the decade leading up to the great plan, counter-movements and reform were fashionable; underground activities instigated global unrest but always yielded little effect. Life itself seemed to prompt humanity to utter some protest against the existing order, but against whom? Who was at fault? Who was to blame? Who trampled the earth, who poisoned the water, who polluted, who spared nothing? Operation Dismantle presumed it was everyone.

* * *

"What shall we call this place?" Alice followed her father down a gentle grass slope to the toppled brick wall behind the garden. Submerged and overgrown with wild grass, it concealed an entranceway mysteriously hidden by ivy and untamed bushes. The ventilator tube's opening, protected by slats, prevented small animals from jumping or hopping down. The pipe head, camouflaged in a bed of shrubs, was visible only to someone who knew it was there.

"Its name?" the father questioned.

"Yes, in case when I wake up, and someone wants to know."

"It's an abandoned fallout shelter," he said. "But no one will ask."

"No one will ask because this is a secret." She liked secrets. Alice watched her father rake back the tangled mat of twigs and foliage. "I didn't even know this was here!" However, her enthusiasm turned to guarded curiosity as he pulled the steel door open, exposing a narrow stairway leading to an underground chamber.

"Wait here," Arbor said. In a few moments, a ceiling fixture illuminated a frosted dome fitting. "You can come down now," he said. "Hold the railing."

It was cool, similar in temperature to a root cellar but without the dampness. Alice took several steps into the room before stopping to observe her new surroundings. Three pods were set against adjacent walls while beside the accessway, a small basin was fastened to the wall, and a pair of metal shelves leaned beside it.

"I see you brought your compass," Arbor smiled as his daughter set the leather pouch on the blanket of a pod bed.

"I remembered." She liked it when her father was pleased and recalled aloud what he had taught her. "I am not to be without a compass because it will be the only mechanical means of indicting direction. In addition, I can look up, and there I will find the north star."

He nodded with approval. "So, what do you think? Cozy, warm enough, and most important, it's safe."

She looked around and shrugged. "It's just like you said it would be. A place to sleep, except it will be for a very long time." She sat down on the edge of the pod and leaned back. "So, you'll be here later," she said, looking over the side. There was a hesitation in her voice, which the father sensed as needing assurance.

"After the plan is executed."

"And mother, when will she be coming to say goodbye."

"You mean, see you later," he corrected. "She'll be here in a few minutes. She's making a picnic lunch. A celebration of new beginnings." Arbor spoke effortlessly as if this was an ordinary day in an ordinary place, but it was anything but ordinary. They weren't going to sleep; they were to be placed in a state of synthetic torpor where physiological activities are reduced, resulting in decreased metabolism, body temperature, heart rate, and respiration to a fraction of their normal rate. Some would call it suspended animation; however, this was an artificially induced state of metabolic suppression.

Alice sat up and crossed her legs. "It's pretty nice in here, and this bed feels okay. I like the blanket, my favorite color of blue." She should have been scared, yet she wasn't. They focused on this day with months of preparation and training. Her parents' instructions stressed that the world would be comparatively antiquated upon her waking up from the long sleep. She was leaving behind a world of technological dependency. Everything she knew would be different, but what they could not foresee was just how much change would take place.

Chapter 8

"*Once the sedative knocks you out, the pod will begin cooling the air around your body. Your core temperature will lower a few degrees each hour, from 98.6°F to below the point of hypothermia. The robotic systems will stimulate your muscles to prevent atrophy.*" Alice smiled, kissed her parents goodnight, and closed her eyes.

Artemis was curiously at ease, considering what had taken place only an hour ago. But there was no need to fill the child's mind with any more details or worries than she needed; Alice was safe, and soon they would all be together. She glanced over at Arbor, who pretended to doze in his chair. His attempt to come to terms with his destiny and the revolutionary events that had befallen him kept haunting his thoughts. His sacrifice to make things globally right was intimately connected with alienation, and he believed the new world order would have no room for them. Other possibilities occurred to him, but he put them out of his mind. He opened one eye and then the other. His wife was staring at him. She smiled and then motioned at the clock.

Arbor was tired of craning behind him to see the time, so he took her gesture as meaning it was just about time.

Artemis glanced at the tastefully furnished room; nothing too bold, simply wood and leather, no plastic or resin. This modest motif presided over all the rooms except the kitchen. That was granite and tile. The hands on the clock had barely moved. "It won't be long," she said.

Arbor pushed the ottoman away with his foot as he sat up. "It will take us approximately four minutes to walk from the back door to the shelter," he said. "And about one minute to rake the entrance door free."

"Then I think we should get started," she concurred. "But how do you know?"

"Know what?"

"How long it will take to walk."

"I timed it."

"What if I walk slower," she asked.

"I took that into account."

"And the raking?"

"Give or take a half-minute."

Artemis decided not to argue about his assuming she would walk more slowly; however, she'd be damned to let him prove her the slower one. Neither had any remorse about leaving the house behind. It was most likely that it would not still be standing when they woke up. Even if it were, it would have new occupants. Everything they would need was already in the shelter, which amounted to the basics: clothes, sealed foodstuff, medicine, toiletries, pencils, paper, a variety of farming and carpentry tools, a rifle, box of ammunition, and a compass. Many having been purchased decades ago in an antique shop.

The sky was stingy with moonlight. Arbor followed his wife to the back wall, where the rake leaned against the pile of bricks. "I feel so small," she said. She stepped back and let Arbor pull the leaves and brush away with the rake. "Do you feel it?" Artemis leaned her chin upward and stared wide-eyed into the night. She was held spellbound by a sort of hypnotic fascination; her gaze riveted on the hive of distant stars. Any regrets were linked in a circle of thought from which there is no escape. The solar superstorm, traveling at a million miles an hour, had broken through Earth's magnetic field with the power of thousands of nuclear bombs detonated simultaneously. The billion-ton monster plasma cloud assailed Earth's magnetosphere with such extreme velocity that the disturbances compressed, distorted, and enhanced the Van Allen belts. It triggered an unprecedented aura of 'northern lights' around the Northern Hemisphere as it passed through Earth's fragile atmosphere. But not a sound was heard as the mother began to grow uneasy with the burden. Choked by a sudden feeling of weakness and fear, she watched as Arbor pulled on the metal door. "We haven't much time," she reminded him. All brave attempts to hide their feelings were betrayed by anxiety, which lined their foreheads and sharpened their words. Arbor continued to pull on the metal handle as the urgency of their situation was eating up precious time.

"What the hell is wrong! Why won't it open?" Artemis's voice cracked as she tried to swallow away her fear.

"It must have automatically locked from the inside; it won't budge! The key, where the hell is the damn key?" But his efforts proved useless as he continued to wrangle with the only object standing between them and destiny.

"The key?" the woman reaffirmed. "It must be inside with our belongings!" Artemis pushed her husband aside and, with all her might, tried to pull it open. "Alice!" she cried and banged her fists on the slatted panels. Filled with despair, she placed her ear against the metal barrier but could hear only her own rapid breathing. "Arbor, what have we done?" Her face displayed fear and bewilderment, and she let her hand fall away from the handle. "We thought of everything," she moaned. She turned and leaned against the metal door. "Everything was perfectly planned," she whispered, and then she began to laugh. "You must admit, we are in a ridiculous predicament. Ironic, isn't it, a damn key, a damn stupid key," she said as if at a confessional.

Arbor shook his head, reluctant to admit defeat. "I'm going back to the garage and find something to break down this door." He turned and looked up towards the sky, wondering if this was his punishment. An unidentified presence tangled inside his gut, and the desert forming in his mouth was giving up on any speech.

"Alice," Artemis cried. "What will Alice do if we don't get inside in time?"

A painful silence stood between the couple, a long mournful moment that forced its way into the brain, slipped behind the eyes, crawled down into the heart, and then, everything went Blank.

Part III

The period of Blank

The details of human frailty, triumphs, sorrows, and tragedies, all information destined for posterity, were erased after the great plan's execution. Past and present facts once faithfully recorded and employed by generations and passed down to the next were gone. This thing called history, consisting of dates and details, chronicled and recounted, could never supply answers to questions; yesterday had become extinct. But perhaps extinct is not the correct word, for to be extinct would imply someone would have information. Maybe the past "was" since it "is" not. Entering the scene is the dawning of present and future. But to behold the future suggests there was a past. So, as you can imagine, life going forward became a curious anomaly for the world's occupants. There were no archives, public consciousness, conditions as they existed, confessions and acknowledgments; any purported truths or fiction was absent. When asked about the past, no one knows, except it is the period of Blank.

Chapter 9

?

???
???
???
???
??? ??????????????????????
???
???
?????????????????????????????? ???
???
???
??????? ???
???
??

???
???
??

???
???
???

???
???
???
???
???
???
???
?? ?????????????????????
???
???
????????????????????????????????????

    ???
???
???
???
???
???????????????????????????????? ??
???
???

    ???
???
???
???
???
??????????????????????????????????????

    ??
???
???

??
?????? ???
??
??? ?????????
??
??
??? ?????????????????????????
??
??
????????????????????????????????

    ??
??
???

    ??
??
??
??
??
??
??
??
??
??
?? ?????????????????????
??
??
??

NANETTE L. AVERY

???
???
???
???
???
??? ????????????????????????????
???
???
??????????????????????????

???
???
???
???
???
?????????????????????? ???
???
??

???
???
??

???
???
???
???
???
???
???
???

BLANK

??
??
??
??
??
??????????????????????????????????????? ???????????????????????????????
??
??
??
??
?? ?????? ?????
??
??
???

??
??
??

Part IV

After Blank (continued)

Chapter 10

Alice was weary and wrapped herself in the shower curtain like a cloak of fine plastic. She lay her head down on the blanket the girls had bought her with the sunflower seeds. It was only a matter of minutes until she fell asleep and began to dream, a fantastic dream that she was in a garden where many gathered. She could not see their faces since all were masked with a veil of gauze, and by the look of their clothes, they must have come from all walks of life. A few wore fine silk coats, and some wore muslin tunics. "What's your name," Alice asked the tallest man in a black silk hat. She liked his hat, although it was a rather odd hat to wear while pulling potatoes. But he only shrugged and shooed her away.

A rat came out from behind the cabbage leaf with some greenery in his mouth, so she waited for him to swallow; otherwise, it would be difficult to understand what it said. "I've never spoken to a rat before," Alice admitted. "Usually, I am quite afraid of your kind."

"As am I afraid of you." The rat grinned and showed its pointy little teeth. "But seeing this is your dream, I suppose we can be friends. However, if you introduce a cat into this dream, we may have to renegotiate our relationship." With that, the rat continued to eat.

"Who is that?" Alice asked the rat, who was now sitting in the shade of the cauliflower flower. She pointed to a veiled woman wearing a pale pink tunic that tipped over her bare feet. The woman was clipping red roses from the bush and laying them into a basket made of woven newspaper.

The rat looked up and thought for a moment. "I believe that is Madame Witt," the rodent said. Alice must have appeared confused to the rat because it offered an explanation without her asking. "The woman has the mind of a judge and bounteous in imagination. You are free to think what you want about Madame Witt though she is filled with reason." Now the rat was tired of talking, or Alice was tired of the rat; either way, it ran away under a newly imagined fence.

"No one can rest with rats about," murmured Madame Witt. The woman bent down over Alice's sleeping self and whispered in her ear, "and to have a garden with a rat roaming about is most futile."

"I'll remember that," said Alice. She was still fast asleep and was in no hurry to wake up. At that very moment, the garden gate opened, and Alice found herself sitting on a bench.

"I am tired from wondering. May I sit with you awhile?" asked the mole. "I think I have lost my way."

"And what way would that be?" The mole was an ugly little creature, but Alice did not wish to hurt its feelings.

"I am not quite sure, you see, I have been hibernating all winter, and when I woke up, I wandered for a bit and came upon this place. The gate was easy to breach, so here I am."

"What do you think of the garden?" Alice asked.

"I'm not sure; I just got here," remarked the mole with disgust for the insipid question. Offended by the mole's curt remark, they sat in silence for several minutes. "You're not much of a thinker, are you?" said the mole squinting from the sun.

"And what makes you say that?" Alice declared. "I should say I have always been a thinker."

"Because critical thinkers take responsibility for their thinking." The mole moved down the bench into the shade. "I suppose you lack critical spirit. Yes," the little fellow affirmed, "perhaps that is what you don't have."

"Critical spirit?" Alice repeated.

"You see, if you had any, you'd know what it was!" smirked the mole, not the least bit sorry for being uncivil.

"Well, if you wish to be rude, then I banish you from this garden."

"You can't!" squealed the mole, "it isn't yours."

"Yes, I can!" threatened Alice. "This is my dream, and you must leave."

The mole shook its head "no," jumped from the bench onto the ground, and then rolled headlong into the carrot bed. By this time, the man in the silk hat moved from the potatoes and meticulously pulled stingy weeds from between carrot plants.

"Have you seen a mole?" Alice asked, quite certain the rude little animal was in proximity of the man.

But the lanky man simply shrugged and went on with his work. Sleeping, Alice watched herself follow the path around the garden until she came to a broken-down brick wall. She tried to remember where she had seen the wall before since it was strangely familiar. "You see," said a voice from behind a pair of stacked bricks. "Critical spirit gives life to reason."

"I'm not here to debate reason with you," sighed Alice to the hidden mole.

"Suit yourself, but if you take my advice, you'll find it."

"Such a flamboyant little animal," Alice thought. "Imagine him taking on the role of sage." The mole rooted around the black earth with his snout, complaining that life was not a picnic. "Father, is this the mole you want me to follow?" Alice heard her awake voice speak as she lay on the blanket of plastic, cold like a codfish, her breathing slow and repetitive. The dream passed over as sleep unfolded like an umbrella. Alice opened her eyes. The garden hut was dark, and she didn't know what time it was. She rolled over on her back, listening to the silence, and remembered she was hungry.

* * *

"I have something to bring over." The old man shaded his eyes with his cap as he raised his face to the woman. He stood sideways against the screen door; her face veiled in shadow. She opened the door and stepped out onto the porch.

"Not a trade?" Doc asked. Their spicy friendship commanded trust in an untrusty world. "Since when are you giving things away?"

"I'm not. More like stashing something for a while," he remarked. He stood with his cap in his hand like a schoolboy.

It was a clear afternoon, and neither the man nor the woman had anything special to do, so she invited him to sit down. "Want some lemonade?" He shook his head no and wondered where she got the lemons from. Her expression was glazed with sincerity.

"Still got those old boots," he said, pointing to her feet. "Always liked them. You got them off that woman ..." He stopped and smiled as his mind drifted back to her guile.

"She didn't need them anymore." The old man nodded in agreement. "So, did you bring it with you?"

The rose water she had bathed in drifted into his nostrils. He suddenly felt ashamed for his thoughts and looked away from where the road stretched beyond his reach. "No." He straightened up and placed his palms on his knees. "It's my grandson."

"Which one?'

"Alabama."

She nodded. "I like that one; he kind of reminds me of you." She could see a smile form around his eyes. "But," she added, "he's a lot better looking than you were." The old man twisted his head and caught her grinning. "When?"

"I was hoping later today. The examiner thought I was going to give him up."

"They are stupid, aren't they," the woman said. "But that's a good thing." They sat for a bit. "I should get a dog," she said.

"Want one? I got a pup ready to leave its Mama."

"One of those smelly hounds?"

"It only smells if it's wet."

"Maybe," she said. "You housebreak it, and then we'll talk."

"That's fair," he said. The old man stood up and stretched. If he stayed too long, it would be painful. Nostalgia could sting, and he didn't want to nurture his feelings with artificial comforts. "Alabama is a good boy; he just needs to be set straight."

"I knew a boy like that, but he never did learn, seemed to get into all kinds of things. Some said he was trouble."

"And you, what did you think?"

"I always did go in for trouble." Doc closed her eyes. "Let the boy know he's welcome." The scent of spearmint drifted past as the man made his way down the steps. The coveted oil was nearly impossible to find. Just the mere smell of the chewed leaves restored her dulled senses, and she opened her eyes. The sky was white, except for the clouds that were very white. The smell of spearmint held fast in her nostrils, and she held her breath as her cultural amnesia was awakening. Why didn't she ever call him by his first name? It wasn't a bad name. "Trenton," she whispered. Something tightened in her windpipe. It took more than nighttime meetings and cunning daytime movement to outwit the enemy. Heroes aren't prominent; they are obscure. The old man had traded his name for secrecy years ago. He was one of the first prisoners to escape. There were disturbances throughout the night, and she knew something was different. He had hidden in the deadhouse until shortly after sunrise when he appeared at her door. *How did you get away? A blaze of blue shot from his sunken eyes when she asked him the question. I can't tell you, he said. She understood but asked him again. Still, he said nothing. Did you kill anyone? However, her prying remained a monologue. She nodded with understanding knowing they would be looking for him. You're hurt, she said, noticing blood on his hands and shirt. Quickly, she ushered him into the house and bolted the door. The awareness of the invaders was always around them.* Now Alabama would appear at her door. There was space enough to harbor the boy, and if he were half the man his grandfather was, he would pass muster.

"He'll be hungry when he gets here; boys his age are always hungry." She took a mental inventory and decided to reheat the mushroom pie. And cheese, there was plenty of yellow cheese. And bread. Yellow cheese, bread, and mushroom pie; that will suit him, and if it doesn't, well, that's too damn bad.

* * *

"Doc's?" The news to Alabama was unwelcome. He acknowledged his harassing the guard, but he bore no responsibility for any other vandalism, even if he did. It's "damnable, unjust, and plain damnable."

"You said damnable twice," the old man reminded him. "It doesn't matter; if you don't do as I say, they'll exile you."

"But Grandpa, Doc's? Couldn't I just say here in the cellar? I could sleep in the cellar." But he knew they would find him, or worse, take away the old man. In the distance, he could hear what sounded like a train. He had always wanted to ride on one.

Two birds appeared at the windowpane; he wasn't superstitious, but birds were rarely seen, especially in pairs. "What should I take?" he asked.

"Enough stuff for a few months until things die down."

"Who will get your tobacco? Nebraska is too young."

The grandfather nodded with agreement. "Looks like I'll have to come by Doc's now and again for a smoke." The boy grinned with the subtle answer. He'd miss the old man.

"When I come back, can we take a train ride?"

"Where to?"

"I don't know," he shrugged. "Anywhere it goes."

"Since when are you so interested in the train?"

"I just thought we could do something different."

"Different isn't always a good idea. First time I saw one speeding down the tracks, it nearly scared the wits out of me."

"Like the first time you saw a puma?" the boy asked.

"Something like that. But a train. The power in those loco-motives, why, there's nothing to compare it with." His voice lingered for a moment as if he had something to add. "Anyway," he said after clearing his throat, "maybe, when you get back. Maybe we could try something different. But until then, don't give Doc any trouble. And, if you think you can fool her, you might as well give it up now."

* * *

"You're going to have to change your name," Danube went on, looking at Alice dubiously. A greater voice in Alice's head asked

What did she say? She said that you'd have to change your name. Well, if that is what she said, then there is no use in answering. Danube and Amazon sat on the floor, looking at her, waiting for her to respond.

"Did you hear what Danube said? You have to change your name," Amazon smiled, trying to appease her with a soothing voice. "It's for your own good." However, with careful examination of the words, Alice shook her head NO. "Now what?" remarked Amazon. "You have to!"

"I don't understand what all the fuss is about over my name. I've been using it all my life, and it still works."

"You have to because it's....!" But Amazon could hardly admit the reason; it was just too mean.

"Too what?" the youth asked.

"It's too weird. You'll get us in trouble with that name," bellowed Danube.

"Oh," sniffled Alice. "I had no idea that it was offensive. Well then, what do you suggest."

"Why not use the name of the place where you were born."

"Moon?" Alice said. "It doesn't sound right. Alice is what I'm used to." The sincerity in her voice was overwhelming.

Amazon stood up, walked over to the small dusty window, and pointed up. "Moon, like up there, in the sky?" she asked. "Listen, Alice; we're not kidding. Where were you born?"

"I am serious, the moon. Look, I can prove it!" And for the first time, she pulled back the short sleeve of her dress to expose the back of her bare shoulder. She twisted her head and pulled her skin forward. "See!"

Danube moved in to get a better look. "It's a star."

"A blue star!" exclaimed Amazon. "How'd you get it."

"I got it when I was a baby. All babies born outside the Earth get one." She pulled her shoulder away and pulled her sleeve down. Then, after a few seconds, she scooted back from the girls who were still leaning into the youth, hoping there were more secrets to see.

"Does it come off?" Danube asked.

"Never, it's on for good. Like your nose!" exclaimed Alice. Amazon laughed at the joke, which Danube did not find very funny.

"Not even with soap?" the younger one asked.

"No, it's body art; why, haven't you ever seen any?" It was apparent that Alice had now diverted the conversation from its original intent into a most curious set of circumstances. The truth of the matter was neither sister knew what to make of all this information, all of which, they decided, was a bald-faced lie. Only the little blue star remained a truth in what Alice perceived as reality.

"How long did you live on the moon?" Danube asked. Amazon giggled at her sister's question, making Alice smile.

"Only a year or so. Then, we moved back to Earth."

"Well, if you don't want to be named Moon, what do you want to be called?" Amazon replied, not wishing to be left out of the conversation. Of all the things about Alice, this was the oddest. The three girls sat cross-legged on the floor, looking one to the other. But there was no utterance of a reply.

"Well, if you don't want to be called Moon, we have no choice but to name you ourselves," Danube decided.

"No, wait, one is coming to me," Alice said. "I am reacquainting myself with another name. Decisions like this take time. You don't just wake up one morning and have your entire world turned upside down without taking time to think. Heavens, it's not every day that someone is rebrandified."

"I don't know what that means," Danube said. Her perplexed expression ignited Amazon, who nodded in agreement.

"It's rebrandification," said Alice. "Presently, I have a perfectly good working identity, but now I must, according to you and Amazon, create a new identity without changing my image. As you can see, it takes careful review." So, she took this moment for deep contemplation by closing her eyes and sitting perfectly still.

The sisters gazed about the shed, sitting not as still, and waiting for Alice to reanimate. Several minutes passed when Alice broke her silence. "Atlantis." Her word, however, was not met with the favor she supposed.

"Atlantis?" Danube repeated as if something tasted sour.

"Why yes. Atlantis, don't you like it?" the youth asked with displeasure in her voice.

"I think it's nice," exclaimed Amazon.

Danube could see she was outnumbered. "Where is it located?"

"I don't know," remarked Alice stretching her legs out in front of her. "No one is quite sure." Both girls rolled their eyes. They had fallen into a word trap. "The best whereabout I can give you is that it is lying somewhere on the bottom of the Atlantic Ocean. It was an island continent, bigger than you could ever imagine!"

"That's all you can tell us!" replied Danube with a sprinkling of disappointment.

"Well, it might be near the Straits of Gibraltar. Anyway, it sank. That's about all I know. Atlantis, it has a nice ring to it, don't you think?"

"Oh, I give up!" Danube said crossly, deciding it would be useless to throw out any suggestions.

"Good!" said the youth considering her words carefully. "Since you insisted that I change my name, I'll be Atlantis; that is until I go back to Alice. I suppose one cannot have too many names." She was thinking about her parents, each having different names for secret occasions, and for a split second, she felt comforted. "As a rule," Atlantis said, "we should have a celebration honoring my rebranding. A party of sorts with a cake and maybe ice cream."

"We don't have any cake or ice cream," said Amazon. "We rarely have dessert."

"Oh, well, that does present a problem," Atlantis remarked. "One can hardly have much of a celebration without cake and ice cream. I guess I'll just have to remain partyless." She paused for a moment to consider the situation. "Well, what can you bring me?"

Danube greeted the question with a scowl. "I must say, you are very bossy! It isn't very nice to ask for things."

"I wasn't asking," Atlantis replied. "I was merely conveying protocol. When one has a birthday, they have a cake; as such, a rebranding is similar in nature. Corresponding to such conventions, cake and ice cream are mandated during celebrations such as these."

"She has a point," Amazon said.

"Except we don't have any!" exclaimed Danube. She was far too exasperated to disagree.

"Well, if that is the case, I will let you both go about your business and let me take my afternoon nap. But, if you happen to find a piece of cake, you have my permission to wake me up!"

Chapter 11

The roads are solitary; the grasses smolder, neglected homes darkly sealed. Following Operation Dismantle, voices were exiled to silence. Beside the brave, the weary sleep, the wounded die, and the enemy appear like a wolf on the fold. The undefined horror arrived like lightning, and it announced fierce acclaims of a new order. To those still living within the city, this was a cry foretelling their destiny. People speak in before-time, colorless and dreamlike, with grumbling floods of complaints. Sophie and Manette could no longer remain. The only possible way forward lay in recognizing a new life away from what was once the Europe they had known. The great plan had been victorious. Every detail on their side had been precisely executed, except the ending. They had awoken from the long sleep to a country in ruins.

On September 17, the ship Sophie Germain and Docteur Manette sailed upon was nearing their destination port. Most of the voyage had been spent in retrospect. Poor Ateka; she thought of the man leaving his dog with her. There was sufficient room in their chamber for the dog. But was there enough oxygen? How could they have been so flagrantly stupid? They were in a hurry; should they, shouldn't they? It seemed too cruel to leave the animal outside, knowing the solar event would erupt at any moment. What a ridiculous idea to risk themselves for the animal.

Her thoughts rose with the tide. The afternoon was a mixture of sun and grey, and she brooded over those indecisions that had checkered several months. Their last contact with anyone from the great plan was an open invitation to Arbor's home. "Join us when you wake up!" Sophie had transcribed the call, keeping the address with their meager belongings. Neither she nor Manette had any intentions of going abroad; until now. But there was no way of letting Arbor and Artemis know about their imminent arrival. Any communication across the ocean was unimaginable, so she could only go on blind faith that their invitation would still be welcomed.

The EU Raju, a four stacked steam engine, was equipped to carry 200 passengers, although fewer than 100 persons, including crew, were aboard. Four others shared their cramped sleeping quarters despite the fact there were half as many wanderers. However, Sophie dared not complain lest she brings attention to herself. But there was plenty to complain about; lousy food, cold water, no privacy; the list could go on and on. Yet, Manette did not seem to mind the other passengers' meddling and found ways to reinvent himself as an architect. His fabrication about Sophie and her need for Inja's companionship appeared to gain universal empathy and not relegate the dog below deck with the other farm animals.

It was a most unlikeable voyage, five weeks of sheer boredom. Mademoiselle Sophie spent most of the time roaming around the deck with Inja in tow while Manette learned a game called checkers. "It's most rudimentary," he told Sophie. "There is a checkered board and two sets of disks, red and black. Each player sits across from one another, and a player is permitted to move one piece. This can involve moving forward to a diagonally adjacent square that is unoccupied or jumping forward over an occupied diagonally adjacent square, provided that the square beyond is also empty. It is really quite amusing, in a primitive sort of way."

"It sounds dreadful," complained Sophie. "I'm not sure I am ever going to get used to our new world."

"Well, we haven't much choice, now do we?" Manette said. "Just think of it as camping."

"For the rest of our lives?" she moaned.

"Yes, more than likely." He offered a smile that was not well received. A well-groomed man dressed in a pale blue suit approached. Pinned to his shirt was a badge with one word, *Official*, printed in large red letters. "We will be docking in about half an hour," he said.

"Should we get our belongs above deck, or will the ship's steward take care of it, Mr. ......?" Docteur Manette was fishing for a name.

"You may call me Aukland."

"Aukland; that is a unique name."

"Not really," he said, restoring the conversation to matters at hand. "Leave all your belongings where they are; there will be time to collect them after inspection."

"Inspection?" Sophie chimed in. "What kind of an inspection." The word stabbed like danger.

"Immigration," Aukland announced.

"Oh, of course," lied Manette, unaware of such matters. "Well, just let us know. We'll be here waiting."

"For our inspection," added Sophie in a less than enthusiastic tone.

"Everyone's inspection," noted Auckland. "Except the dog," he said, pointing at Inja. There was scarcely a ripple of a smile, although his eyes seemed to soften as he ventured to gaze at the dog. Then, the man nodded and shuffled off to the next pair of travelers leaning against the railing.

"Merde," whispered Sophie.

But Manette ignored her pessimism and turned his head to watch Auckland and the passengers' interactions. A bit of jocularity seemed to pass between the strangers, and then after a moment or two, the Official sauntered away.

They sat for more than an hour when a singsong voice emitted a single continuous word. "Attention, attention, attention." The ship docked, and the lowered gangplank greeted the arrival of immigration inspectors. "Attention, all passengers are required to report to the mess hall. All passengers report to the mess hall."

"Well, this is nice. Supper before we disembark," declared Docteur Manette. "Hear that, Sophie, supper."

"I'm afraid not," glowered a stout gentleman overhearing the remark. "You've had your last meal aboard this tub. That is unless you're headed back to your home port."

"No supper?" replied Sophie. Her day was already filled with enough disappointment. But the stout gentleman did not hear, having hurried ahead and stood in a queue that wrapped around the entire corridor when they arrived.

* * *

Inja sat under a table, watching as the line of people grew shorter. She rested her head on her front paws, not taking her eyes from Sophie until the woman exited through the doorway. But rather than napping, she set her sights on a man carrying a duffle bag balancing a long loaf of bread under his arm. The dog licked her chops and waited, hoping the bread would drop. But, unfortunately, it didn't, and the man lumbered to the outside deck with the weight of his bag hitting his leg and Inja sneaking close behind.

The passengers were directed to a dining table covered with a white linen cloth inside the dining hall. Seated behind the table was a pair of grim-appearing officers sent from the immigration field office. Each wore a dark green uniform and cap to match. Both men were bearded, one grey, the other grey too. Unlike what was expected, however, they were unusually pleasant. "We're sorry about this morning's wait. We just need to get down a few things," Commander Canberra remarked in a more than casual tone. "Candy?" He lifted a glass bowl of wrapped sweets.

"No, no, thank you."

"They are very good," Officer Cairo said. And helping himself, he offered up one from his palm to Sophie.

"Then let's get started. "Who will you be staying with?"

"We're not quite sure yet," Sophie said, shaking her head as she declined the offer of candy.

"And jobs, what jobs have you lined up?" Commander Canberra asked.

"Well, I thought I would pursue the availability of an architectural position," Manette replied, noticing the Commander picking through the candy dish as he listened.

"Well, look, Cairo, a sour ball."

"Looks like your lucky day. And it's a red one, cherry," Officer Cario said with envy.

"And I may look into dog walking," the Mademoiselle interrupted, seeing as they would be asking her the same question.

"Dog walking?" Commander Canberra asked with a sizeable amount of puzzlement in his voice. "Can't they walk themselves?" he chuckled. "All dogs on this side of the Atlantic are very adept at walking."

"What she means is that she will be caring for dogs. Like a dog babysitter," Manette explained, trying to qualify the answer.

An awkward moment surrounded the applicants as a few papers were shuffled. Cairo stroked his beard and shrugged. Then he pointed to a paragraph and held his finger above a line. "No," he said and then looked up.

Commander Canberra repeated the surprising answer. "I will have to agree, no."

"No what?" insisted Docteur Manette.

"No, you may not gain entry." He seemed pleasantly satisfied, although a bit remorseful that the two emigrants traveled all this way only to return from where they came.

Horrified, Sophie shuddered with disgust. "No, no, you say, and why not?"

"Simply because you will add nothing to the existing population. Frankly, you haven't anything to offer," Officer Cairo said regretfully. "Now, had you made accommodations or had a useful occupation, like a plumber, or mason, then perhaps we could get you in on a work visa. By the looks of your hands, I can see, Sir, you haven't done much work. And you, Ms. Sophie, a dog walker? You couldn't have come up with a more ridiculous trade. All dogs in the occupied territory are working animals." The officer laughed and unwrapped a toffy.

"Occupied?" Docteur Manette questioned.

"Indeed, you must know about the temporary transfer of sovereignty?" remarked Cairo. "Then again, you have been on the other side of the ocean. Now, if you would not mind, I need to process many other travelers." He smiled warmly and handed Sophie a stamped form. "If you give the steward this paper, he will help you get resettled. At least you won't have to change ships."

"Isn't there anyone we can appeal to?" asked Sophie. But with that question, Docteur Manette pulled her away.

"Don't be a damn fool," he whispered. "You heard what they said, occupied. The United States is occupied, overthrown, maybe even turned into a colony! Who knows what it's like out there!" He looked gravely at the woman.

"Well, I must get Inja before we return to our deck," she exclaimed, and nearly tripping over the coaming, she parted company with Manette in a great hurry. Believing the dog was nearby, she called; however, Inja did not follow her voice, unlike all other times. Sophie paced nervously up and around the deck, peering under deck chairs and looking into forbidden cabins. It wasn't until she arrived at the gangway when a respectable-looking gentleman stopped her. "I am sorry, Mama," the Purser asserted, "but you are not permitted to exit." He stood between a pair of shaggy-looking potted plants, all of which were blocking Sophie's egress.

"You must let me by," she said, hoping to appease the man's good nature. "It's my dog; I think she may have gone down the gangway."

"What does it look like?"

An odd question, Sophie thought, how many dogs do they get leaving? A tan dog with a long fluffy tail.

"Tall or short?"

"I suppose tall. But not too tall, and yes, Inja was wearing a red leather collar."

The man smoothed his brown mustache as he contemplated. "I did see a dog fitting that description leave. But he was not alone."

"Not alone!" Sophie squealed. "Then someone has stolen my dog!"

"Oh no, Mama, I would have to disagree. The dog left on its own accord and did not appear to be in any distress. It just so happened that the dog was shadowing an elderly fellow with a large valise. I believe the animal was in pursuit of the man's possession, a loaf of bread nested under his arm."

"This is terrible," Sophie lamented. "I must get Inja back!"

"Well, Mama, the only thing I can do is make out an incident report and give it to the authorities onshore. Perhaps they will be able to locate the lost cat. In the meantime, I must ask you to go back up to your deck."

"It's a dog, you damn fool! Haven't you been listening? My dog is gone!"

"Well, you needn't be rude, Mama. I merely got my animals confused. Here, you see, I am writing it down. DOG." And with his finger, he traced the word on his outstretched palm. "I will not forget; it is embedded in my person."

"A reward, I can offer a financial reward for his return!" exclaimed Sophie.

"I am afraid you don't have anything anyone would want, but your sentiments are noted." He drew his face inches towards hers and whispered, "Please, do not make a scene." He slowly backed away and motioned for her to leave, uttering a long peevish pause under his breath.

Inja was gone, gone forever. She passed through the corridor and wondered how cold the ocean water might be.

Chapter 12

Alabama peered through the window, but it was too dirty to see inside clearly. He rubbed his elbow against the dusty pane but managed only to smudge the grime over the glass. He wanted to tell the girl he was leaving. He wondered if she would care. The bouquet of clover gathered on his way to the shed was wilting in his sweaty palm. He found the door ajar and lightly pulled it open a bit wider. She was sitting upon a stool with her head bowed. Her hands cupped her forehead, oblivious to his entry. The shed was damp, smelling musty, all the same imparting a quaint coziness. Perhaps it was the lighting. A hint of umber filled the space, casting a solemn light over the girl. He knocked lightly on the door and waited. Alice looked up, her eyes caught him, and she smiled. "Where's your brother?" she asked.

"I'm alone."

"I'm never alone," Atlantis said and turned to see the flowers hanging limply in his hand. "Those are pretty," she said. "Who are they for?"

It was a strangely odd question, he thought, but she was strangely odd. "You," he replied. "I thought maybe you'd like a bunch. They're clover." He put his hand out towards her, and she bowed her head to smell them.

"Oh, nice," she exclaimed. "Thank you." She jumped down from the stool and walked over to the rack. Rummaging around for a moment, she spotted a tin cup and dropped the clover in it, leaning them to one side of the vessel. "You can now call me Atlantis," she said.

"Not Alice?"

Alice, having surrendered her name, asked, "Do you like the name Atlantis?" Her question offered him no room to disagree.

Alabama nodded, "Sure, it's fine." She grinned, not sure if he was telling the truth. "I guess you're wondering why I'm here."

"To get some seeds, I imagine. Help yourself. I always do." She turned her back on Alabama as she began to rearrange the jars, placing them in size order. "It seems as though there are a lot of sunflower seeds. I have counted over half a dozen jars. Actually, it was Alice that counted them. I can only take her word for it." She could feel his presence behind her and hesitated to turn, fiddling with a container marked "sesame."

"I came by to tell you I have to go away." His voice resonated in her ears. All she heard was the word "away."

"Away?" she repeated and turned around. "Away to another place? Because if you were going "a way," that would not be sad. If you don't have "a way" to get to your destination, then you couldn't go away, now, could you?"

Alabama laughed. "You have a point. No, I am leaving. I am going away."

"Then that is sad." She decided he was nice; she liked him.

He stood with his hands in his pockets, looking as if he had just come in for supper. "I can try to sneak out and visit you," he suggested.

"Can you tell me where you'll be, I won't tell anyone except Alice, and she knows now anyway."

"Doc's."

Atlantis stepped closer. She was wearing the dress Danube had given her and suddenly felt very cold. The day seemed like night, and she yearned for sunshine. "I hope you will be safe. It's good to feel safe," she admitted. He was young but not too young to do important things. She saw him in a new light. "You can do great things, she said. "You don't have to surrender to their ways. Claim memories before the occupiers make them for you."

Alabama listened and wondered where she had learned so much self-confidence. She had knocked on his door and, without realizing it, broken in. No one had done that before. He wanted to reach out and hold her hand, only he hesitated. "What about you?" Alabama asked. "It's terrible to feel isolated, all alone in this shed."

"I'm not alone; there's Alice. Anyway, nothing stays the same forever, but for me, it has. But you, Alabama, you can do wonderful things. I have to follow the mole."

"Follow the mole?"

"Yes, it's a little rhyme Alice's parents taught her. Listen while I tell you the secret of fairy rings."

Along the lonely countryside
Golden wheat grows shoulder high
Where Mr. Mole makes fairy rings
And up above the blackbirds sing
He burrows tunnels all around
Building homes beneath the ground
His favorite game is hide and seek
Find him at the old mill creek
Travel at an easy pace
Until the stones are out of place
Look to the east and down split logs
Part the reeds to see the frogs
Follow the mole where the old creek falls
And red vines climb over stony-walls

"It sounds like a puzzle," Alabama remarked.

"Yes," agreed Atlantis. "I'm sure Alice knows what it means."

There was solace in the shed, and he understood why Alice would not want to leave. Outside, the world was harsh. The youthful girl offered him understanding that he readily accepted. Her remarks framed a different view from his; she made ordinary words come alive. "I saw something I think you would like," he suggested. "But you'll have to go outside to see it."

"That's fine," Atlantis said. "I walk to the outhouse even without a full moon."

"What I want to show you is not too far off the path," he added and opened the door. Atlantis followed as Alabama led the way through weedy patches of scrub grass and pointed to the intended direction of his secret. "Just over there." Confined within the woodland, they came upon rings of loose soil. Alice bent down and ran her hand over the earth. "These are fairy rings," she whispered.

Alabama signaled to the left. "Those look newer." A line of small mounds was the result of more unearthed soil.

Alice brushed the soil off her hands. "They like to play hide and seek," she said. Her crooked mouth smiled, and she laughed with genuine delight.

Time belonged to no one, but Alabama was conscious of losing it. "I better take you back to the shed," he announced with a disappointed voice. He took her hand, and they walked back in silence to the shed.

A cloud veiled the sun and a cooler than usual breeze brushed against the door, swinging it open. In a few moments, she would be inside. "Do you want to kiss me goodbye?" she asked.

The unexpected question needed no response. "Will I be kissing Alice or Atlantis?"

But she didn't wait to answer and raised her chin. His hair fell over his brow as he brought his face towards hers. The gentle kiss was the first line of a poem, and when he left, she hoped he would return.

* * *

Alabama set his suitcase down and knocked. The woman opened the door and looked at him indifferently through the screen. But even an alley cat needs to be treated with affection, and just shy of a warm welcome, she invited him in. "So, you're Alabama. Well, come on in. I imagine you must be thirsty."

"Thank you, I am," he said, pleased she didn't find him to be objectionable. He followed her through the foyer and into the hallway, where he stepped through the threshold into the kitchen. There was a stillness about the room that he found immediately comforting. The kettle, the checkered tablecloth, even the iron skillet on the stovetop offered a sentiment he was not used to. The flour canister, pickle jar, and spice boxes were aligned in size order; even her gingham apron hanging on a peg looked tidy. All things were in their place.

"I'm Doc, not sure if your grandfather ever mentioned me before. He told me about your trouble." She took a clean glass from the shelf and poured him a glass of milk. "I only have one rule, act appropriately. If you can follow that, we'll get along famously." She smiled and handed him the glass. "You can sit down; I imagine you are a bit tired."

"Maybe a little, Ma'am." He pulled out the chair from the table and rested his suitcase next to his legs.

"I can see you aren't a trusting soul. Well, I can understand that. But you don't have to worry. You're safe here." She lifted the valise and set it by the open door. "And one more thing. Call me Doc; if you call me Ma'am, I feel like my grandmother. Not that that's a bad thing," she added with a smile.

"O.k., Doc," he said, glancing up. She sat down across from him, passing several idle minutes in their own thoughts.

"Trenton tells me the authorities are after you." It was an awkward way to start a conversation, Alabama thought. He took the last gulp of his milk and got up to rinse his glass in the sink. "Just set it aside and come sit down," she said. He turned to look at her over his shoulder and did as she said, setting the glass in the sink. His mind drifted like a rowboat downstream, gently switching from side to side. He glanced at the suitcase and then at the door. Doc sat attentively waiting while he settled back into his seat. "I just want to know what to say and what not to say if they come knocking, that's all."

"All I did was pitch a rock up at the sentry in the guardhouse. I suppose my aim was pretty good because his head fell off." He grinned, vowing never to reveal it was Nebraska's perfect aim. He would protect his little brother at all costs.

"Head fell off?" Doc's voice wavered with the question.

"We weren't sure until we snuck back to see. It was knocked to the ground, and pieces shattered and tossed around." Doc expelled a sudden sigh of relief.

"I don't think you understand what you've done," she started to explain. "Those robotic guards were the last of their kind. You've managed to destroy one of the only automata still around. Those buffoons in the guardhouse probably don't have a clue as to what they were using. Naturally, the authorities are looking for you. Who else besides your brother was with you?" Alabama hesitated; he wasn't sure if he would be a snitch if he told. Doc read his mind; he wasn't the first person to try to take the entire wrap for someone else. "It's okay; your secrets are safe with me; I've got my own baggage to tend to without hanging out your dirty tales."

"It was me, Nebraska, and Amazon."

"The River's girl?"

"Yes, but she just wanted to see. I think it was kind of a dare."

Doc nodded, exploring all implications that might ensue. There was no appealing to the authorities. He would be sent off to a remote work farm or become part of a chain gang. A boy of his youthful looks and age would be subject to abuse. "As long as you're not interrogated, no one would implicate the others. For now, you can stay here until we sort things out." He hated that term, "sort things out." There was nothing to sort out; he was a fugitive, and what Doc was offering, he didn't want. He wondered if he could trust her or if he should navigate around her words. But he didn't know where he would go, so for now, he would stay. It was unrealistic to take off without a plan. A plan, everyone needs a plan. "How good are you at reading?" she asked.

The question bristled. "I can read and write if that's what you're asking," he replied.

"Good, that's one thing you won't have to worry about." She went on. "If you get picked up and can't read, you will immediately be placed into hard labor. But, on the other hand, readers are considered useful and are often treated more humanely." Alabama swallowed away a lump forming in his throat. He was a man in a boat without a rudder.

"Isn't that discrimination?" he retorted.

"The authorities don't give a damn about fairness or rights. We are part of the machine, a system that is fueled on the output of workers." Her words, spoken with a gentle tongue, assembled in his thoughts like a prophecy. His world was closing over him, and he didn't know what to do. He couldn't let his spirit be dismembered, nor his head swing from the rope of the gibbet. Doc's warning excluded disappearances and assassinations. "What do you want to be?" she asked. He paused and thought for a moment. The worst part of the question was he didn't know or know how to answer. He shrugged. "Well, you don't want to be a gatherer all your life. You're put on this Earth to do more."

"No, I'm not going to be a gatherer forever. I just don't know right now."

"Tell me," she asked again.

Tell her what? He was deluded by uncertainty. "I'm not sure."

"Everyone has something they want to do," she pressed.

"I've never been asked." The idea that there were choices was buried in the most remote part of his brain, and suddenly, such a concept tempted him. Ever since he could remember, choices were dictated, and individual decisions suppressed.

"Do you understand that not making a choice is a choice? A choice isn't something tangible, like an apple; instead, it's a power you use to select between one outcome or another." Outcome, decision, power, choice; the mere exhale of these words could bring trouble. And now, he wondered what Doc was suggesting. What was she up to? Could she be testing him, his loyalty to the occupiers, to the Supreme Potentate? "There will come a time when you learn how to choose," she said, looking directly into his eyes. "You look tired." Her voice sounded more subdued, and he wanted to believe her and the things she preached. She pointed to his bag by the door. "Take your belongings and follow me;

there's a cot and a dresser in the garret. You can sleep up there. It's small but clean, and the mattress is soft. I put out an extra blanket because sometimes it can get chilly. You may use the bathroom on the floor below." She stood up, resting her hands on the back of the chair. Alabama didn't know what to make of her, but he had to believe his grandfather knew what he was doing, leaving him here. There was pure silence in the room now except for a bird's trill entering through the open window. Such a sound was rare, and Doc sensed his appreciation for the bird. "I know it's illegal to do, but I leave some seed for the birds," she explained. "Even winged creatures have to eat too."

Chapter 13

If Elijah Ateka had known Sophie would be so careless with his dog, he might not have given it over to her that sultry afternoon. However, he would never know because the unfortunate man did not return home as intended. Instead, the plane he was scheduled to embark upon had been delayed due to bad weather, the same inclement weather that caused his untimely demise.

Standing outside beneath the airport overhang, Ateka smoked a cigarette. In the distance, he could see the runway where grey clouds lay low and heavy. Another waiting passenger asked him for a light. Without hesitation, he reached into his pocket to retrieve the lighter when a stronger than usual gust of wind blew in their direction, stripping the metal awning off its frame and striking both men. A crowd of onlookers circled, a woman felt faint, and in a matter of moments, Ateka was carried away, never to regain consciousness.

* * *

Inja kept her nose to the ground, sniffing and stopping to investigate unfamiliar objects. And being a dog, she used her instinctive abilities to root out anything edible. All things fitting into this category were immediately consumed. The dog's new surroundings did not appear to cause her any undue harm, so she went about her business with little on her mind except food. She crossed an iron bridge that spanned the river, but had she followed it to the road; she may have continued on a safer route. Instead, her thirst directed her decision to crisscross down the rocky bank until she came to the muddy shoreline. Unfortunately for Inja, a canine of her proportions and pedigree were rare and had the potential of bringing someone a great deal of currency, which was precisely the intention of a pair of anglers when they saw her approaching.

"Well, I have never seen a canine-like that one!" exclaimed Fairfax. The old woman eagerly pointed at the dog lapping the muddy water.

The gaunt friend with sunken eyes turned to see and smiled. "We could sell it at the market, with our fish," she declared. "But how do we catch it? I'm just a broken old woman and look at the size of the beast."

"Nonsense, Arcadia, as long as we have more wits than that dog, we'll find a way to take her home with us." She paused to think as the other pulled in her line to examine the river-grass caught on the hook. "Give me your sash," Fairfax said, "and with mine, I'll tie them together like a rope. See, it's wearing a collar; lucky for us; it's such a fancy dog."

Reluctantly, Arcadia removed her blue sash, handing it over to her friend. "Now what?" asked the woman, wary of the animal. "It's got some big teeth. Maybe we should leave it be. We're just two poor women." The dog's soft tan fur was stained with mud, and she was busy poking her nose into pockets of water-filled holes. "Oh, look at her, so dirty. No one will want a dirty dog."

"We do," whispered Fairfax. "Put down your pole and come with me. All we gotta do is call it over; if she's a good dog, we'll tie this to her collar." She held up the sashes and grinned.

"And if she's bad, she'll bite us!"

Inja scampered up and back with a sweeping tail, chasing the rolling tide, unaware of the approaching women. Fairfax dangled the sash trying to bait the playful dog, yet it didn't pay any attention to the old woman or her soggy sashes. Timidly, the old woman called "Here pup!" which caught the ear of Inja. But seeing it was just a dirty-looking rag instead of something to eat, the dog quickly escaped its nemesis, leaving the women shouting profanities she did not understand.

For the rest of the hot afternoon, Inja slept in the shade of the iron bridge, too tired and too disinterested to investigate. Her life had once been easy for a dog, and the burden of looking for food and shelter would soon make her an easy mark. For even a dog can become complacent. Such was the downfall of Inja. Luck went her way with the two old anglers; however, as the afternoon grew into twilight, out with the evening comes more than stars.

The window of the boatbuilder's hut looks out on the river's pines. His wife, a woman calling herself Dorsey, raised the evening lantern up to the pane between the trees. A ritual she performed every evening that beckoned her husband, Andes, to dinner. She turned the dial back and forth, lowering and raising the flaming wick, after which she would place it on the table and go about her business. But today, she stopped and peered more closely. In the near distance was the silhouette of her husband and a four-legged creature. The enormous size of the animal appeared like a figment of her imagination. She remained vigil as the man and beast disappeared from view. Naturally, the clueless woman believed her husband was in danger, and she chastised him for his bravado actions. Little did she know, he was leading a gentle dog that would soon bring her a small bit of revenue.

* * *

The dog remained tied up outside the hut for two days. Dorsey brought Inja water and filled a tin plate with fish and potato peelings scraps. At first, Inja reluctantly moved the offerings around with her nose, but after finding neither the boat-builder nor his comely wife brought anything else to eat, Inja reluctantly obliged. She slept on a bed of pine needles, and in the late afternoon when Andes arrived home, he walked her on a short lead around the hut. Though it was only two days, Inja had become miserably sullen. "Don't look so displeased," Andes told the dog. "Our life is nothing but drudgery. Maybe your next owner will feed you something you like. But until then, be happy with what you get." But two more days passed, and now it was a total of four days chained to a post. It wasn't until the fifth day that Andes led her down to the river for a bath. "If I had a use for you, I'd let you stay with Dorsey and me, but we haven't any use for a dog with your appetite." It was the first time someone spoke gently, so she wagged her tail.

* * *

Doc moved along the road toward the stockade. A long string of onlookers leaned against the wooden barriers. A rickety shebang held up a thatched roof made from a web of branches, good enough to keep the animals cool until they were brought out. Most of those waiting were shoeless and tired gatherers who had arrived early to get a good viewing location. A dozen voices were bantering among themselves, in tones secretive and suspicious in nature. Each seller had one minute to convince the buyers to consider their animal. When their time was up, the bidding would begin. It was risky for the sellers since profits were shared between themselves and the government. If no one wanted their animal, they would still have to pay a tax for the use of the stockade. Most of the buyers gathered in hopes of purchasing a laying hen, chicks, or a cow. On this day, a mule was rumored to be available. "But who could keep a mule?" whispered a young man to his wife. She smiled and envied the family that could afford such a grand animal.

A uniformed guard slowly walked from the shebang to the center of the stockade and, with a raised hand, pressed his palm to the crowd, gesturing silence. Then without uttering a word, he pointed to the overhang and motioned for the first seller to come forward. A youth and his sister brought forward a box and set it on the ground. Gingerly, the girl lifted the lid and placed her hand into the box, lifting a large and very ornery-looking cat. Most of the crowd laughed and heckled the children until the young boy called out loudly, "It's a ratter. And I guarantee, if you buy our cat, you'll never be unhappy."

"What's its name?" jeered a rusty bearded man.

"Vesuvius!"

"How much are you asking for this ratter?" another asked.

"A bag full of sunflower seed."

"Give you half-a bag!" countered the bearded fellow.

"Three-quarters!" cried a woman, pushing against the crowd to see.

"No," frowned the sister and kissed the howling cat on the head before shutting it back into the box.

"Three bags!" A voice from the crowd cried.

"Three?" the youth exclaimed. "You want him for three?"

"That's what I said. Bring Vesuvius here to me if you want your three bags," demanded Doc. Around the stockade was a gleeful murmur. Such an offer was more than generous; it was stupid. "I don't suppose you have a dog?" she asked the children as they approached with the box. She handed the three bags of seeds and accepted the howling cat.

"Vesuvius doesn't like being in the box," the little girl explained. "If you want to make him happy, be sure to give him milk."

"And you be sure to look in the bags I gave you," remarked Doc. "They could be filled with sand. One can never be too careful when making a business deal." She watched as the children untied the pouches and nodded with acknowledgment. "Now, a dog? I wanted a dog and not a cat."

"Then why did you buy him?" The youth, quite confused, was making little sense from this strange woman.

"I bought him as a gift," she explained. "Ratters make excellent gifts for cat lovers. Myself, I want a dog. A large dog. I don't suppose you know of anyone selling a dog?"

There was a moment of contemplation, and as the cat yowled, Doc swayed the box as if she were rocking a baby to sleep. But to no avail, the animal was in no mood to be soothed. "Down by the iron bridge, I saw a dog about a week ago. It was tied up at the boatbuilder's. Maybe it's still there."

Doc eyed the boy with skepticism. Dogs wandering about were extremely unusual. However, she had nothing else to do today. "Don't you two think you had better be getting home with all that currency?"

A single "yes" was spoken by both. The youth took the three pouches and tucked them into his shirt, patting the bulge for good luck. "Well, thanks, lady. Take care of Vesuvius; he's a great ratter."

"May I say goodbye to him," the teary-eyed little girl requested as she placed her face to the box and whispered something to the noisy cat.

"Oh, I think you can do better than that," explained Doc quite unexpectedly. "Take him back home and do not return to this dreadful place ever again."

"For me?" the child asked.

"Anyone that needs to sell their beloved Vesuvius needs the seeds more than I do. I bought the cat for you. I have no use for a ratter, and in fact, I am not fond of the feline species. They are too much like me," she laughed. "Now, take your cat, the seeds, pay the tax, and be gone." It pleased Doc to see the children happy, one clutching the box and the other dolling out seeds to pay the tariff. Not every story ends happily like this one.

* * *

Doc decided to trust the youth and started on her way toward the iron bridge. Her life was becoming more complicated than time allotted; however, her promise to keep Alabama safe needed more than her assurance. She needed an extra measure of safeguarding without drawing attention to herself. A notice of a dog's sighting was posted throughout the territory, so the boatbuilder possibly saw it. The advantage Doc had over most was her wealth. A broad brush is needed if one wants to paint with broad strokes.

The smell of gutted fish and cigars dominated the trail that led to the iron bridge. It had been more than several months since she had ventured to the river, and as she walked made a promise to herself to go this way more often. Despite the smell, she liked the water. This was an annexed area outside her territory not well patrolled. Those living by the water paid taxes for the rights to use the river. For Doc, it seemed unlikely that any beaver trappers, fishermen, or boatbuilders would keep a dog. More likely, it would have been sold in the black market. All of which gave Doc reason to believe she could negotiate if the dog were still alive.

On the sandy bank, the line of pine trees, like a small forest, hid any human encounter, and although Doc saw no one, she felt she was being watched. Then, as if stones skipped along the water's surface, a settled calm sounded, and when she looked outward, she noticed it was only the fish jumping. She followed the bend for a few more yards and stopped. Out from the pines, a man walked towards the shore. He was not a threatening-looking fellow, but his gait was sharp and quick. He was smoking a cigar, and when he came closer, she could see he had a knife in his sheath. "We don't get many strangers around here," he announced.

"But I'm not a stranger. Maybe you are," Doc replied. In the shadows of the pines, she could see he was not alone. A large and morose-looking dog was tied to a tree trunk by a long rope. It followed behind the man and stopped when there was no more length on its rope. "Fisherman?" she asked.

"Boatman, actually builder of vessels," he replied. The dog whimpered and lay down. "Found this one along the river," he said, pointing to Inja. "Not much to look at but might be of some good to someone. My wife said I should take it to the market, but I don't have the heart."

"No?" inquired Doc. "I didn't take you for a soft-hearted man."

"Not soft-hearted. "

"A revolutionary?" Doc questioned.

"You could say that. I was part of the last insurgency. And you?" he asked cautiously.

The woman nodded. "TY-125."

"Me, TY-136. But that was almost a decade ago," he said. "So, what are you doing in this area, aside from walking," he laughed.

"I heard about the dog."

"How?" His inquiry sounded like a complaint.

"A flyer is posted." She chose not to mention the youth.

"Damn them. I should have expected that."

"Indeed," agreed Doc. "I can take her off your hands. I could use a big dog."

"Yes? But I can't just give her away, even if you are a fellow TY." The allegiance to the cause had struck a nerve.

"What would you take for a trade?" Doc asked, not wishing to overpay.

"Make me an offer," Andes countered.

"Alfalfa. Say three-quarters of a pound."

"Alfalfa?"

"Yes, freshly dried. I have it with me in my bag. So, naturally, I'll take the dog now, and that will be the end of our transaction." She looked carefully at his eyes, scrutinizing his expression. "And don't tell me your name," she added. "No names mean no trouble."

"My wife will be pleased with your offer. She wasn't taking to my keeping the dog." Doc lifted a cloth pouch from her bag, pinched out some alfalfa seeds, and sprinkled them into his palm. "Nice," he said, running his fingers over the clump. He smiled contently, his breath stinking from the cigar. "I think I got the better deal," he said.

"Then we're both happy," Doc agreed. "And maybe even the dog."

Doc handed over the alfalfa seeds and watched as Andes stuffed them into his pocket. "Now that our business is over," she began, "I will candidly talk since I feel you are trustworthy. There are rumors of new arrivals."

Andes faced the words with mechanical attention. "That so?"

She nodded. "If so, then we won't be the only ones who know this."

"True," he said with disgust.

"Rumors are scarcely facts, but I have enough information to believe my sources are most likely correct. I can send someone around if I find anything else. If that's alright with you, TY-136."

"Do it. We should be prepared, unlike the last time, if there is to be a next time."

Doc walked over to the dog and, without looking back, untied the rope from around the tree. "Then I will count on you," she remarked. "There will be a next time."

Chapter 14

I t's not your choice, the first road you travel. Some are sandy and difficult to walk on, while others are rocky or etched with ruts. On the way, we pick up hitchhikers, some keep up, and others weigh us down. The roads lead up, down, backward, or remain a dead end. We are left with mud or dirt on our shoes that we try to pick away and wipe off, but it persists, a hard coating or fine veneer. We will never know when the journey ends until we are suddenly there.

* * *

The old man never lifted his head from the pillow. He was still, listening to the wind rattle the loose shutter boards. He wondered if he was the only one who could hear it, and then he remembered he was alone with Nebraska. A wheezing cough interrupted his rest. He wasn't sure how long he had been asleep. An hour, a day?

"You've been asleep for 15 hours," Nebraska said.

"How do you know," the old man asked. "You can't tell time." He knew he had hurt the boy and suddenly felt sorry.

"The doctor was here."

"Doctor, that old quack. Who asked him to come?"

But Nebraska didn't answer because the old man had suddenly drifted off in a wakeful sleep. He was right; the doctor was useless. But they all were. Nebraska peered over his grandfather and touched the wrinkled forehead. The man's body radiated heat. He dipped a piece of muslin into a shallow pan of cold water and wrung it out before laying it on the forehead. The old man twitched and then opened his eyes. "Did he give me anything for this scratchy throat? It's like I got a piece of cactus stuck down there."

"He made up some elixir, Grandpa. Don't you remember, you said it tasted like manure!"

The old man winked, "Yes, now I remember." Then he closed his eyes.

The bedroom was thick with the stale air of a dying man, and Nebraska was afraid. He took his grandfather's hand and held it lightly so as not to wake the resting man. Then he lay it on the bedsheet. If the old man died, it would be his fault. He needed help but didn't know who to ask or where to go. The old man wouldn't tell him where Alabama was taken. He said it was for his own good that he couldn't get in trouble for lying if the authorities came asking. "You stay here," the boy told the old hound. The dog opened one eye and then went back to sleeping on the foot rug. Nebraska got up and went downstairs to look at the clock. The doctor told him to give him more elixir in five hours. He counted two hours more.

* * *

"There is no trace of Father or Mother, alive or dead," Alice reminded Atlantis. "But, not located does not authenticate never located, and so, they are simply late. And because they are rarely, if ever, late, we can assume something has detained them." The explanation suited Atlantis. However, Alice, the more pragmatic ego, was not convinced by her rationale. Alice's secret trips back to the garden only made herself ever more doubtful of her parents' success to pass through Blank. But she would never tell Atlantis, who now was becoming more like the present company, reactionary. Alice was second-guessing whether rebranding was a good idea; her emotions were getting in the way of clarity.

What transpired since her exiting the sleeping pod needed a severe amount of sorting out. She was indeed lost, unable to identify with the here and now, this strange place everyone called "Occupied." As though a seashell had washed ashore from another land, she stuck out from the other shells that were smooth and conformed in shape. Instead, Alice thought of herself more as a shell-picker, scrutinizing and gathering until finding one that was more like herself.

Her parents had spoken, they had followed a mandate, waged a just war, and she followed the prescription provided. The followers of "Operation Dismantle" addressed problems. Their obstinate refusal to allow the status quo to continue was conducted without indulging in physical violence. However, as Alice was now trying to reconcile, the responsibility for current conditions worldwide rested with their involvement. After Blank, unchronicled events of the past remained unknown. Aggression unleashed, and political turmoil ensued. Alice sat on the stool and thought. "What would her parents think if they were with her?" Worldwide economic infrastructures had broken down, and totalitarian governments like sharks smelled blood. Invaders advanced from the sea, took up positions, and struck. It was a game of cat and mouse, and the cat won.

Alice was not familiar with the story of why so many countries collapsed. She was unaware of the chaos and turmoil that came with occupation; she was unaware of the noose holding tight around what was once a democracy. All she could tell was the reins of power had slipped away. She was cold and pulled the plastic sheet over her shoulders. Even so, she liked the garden shed. It belonged to her, and she felt no desire to leave. It was, after all, on her property. The Rivers family were the trespassers, not her. But she decided she'd let Artemis and Arbor sort it out when they arrived, which she reminded Atlantis might not be very soon.

Alice was born on the moon. She had little recollection of living there except for a few memories of the playroom. It was a large, well-ventilated children's room with a window facing the north crater and blanched ruble landscape. It had brightly decorated wall coverings since everything outside was stark and grey. When she arrived on Earth, she was four years old. She attended the neighborhood school where the curriculum followed a general reading and writing course, sciences, history, art, physical education, and technological practices. Her parents supplemented her schooling with a healthy dose of ecology and outdoor survival skills. Little did she know they were training her for their future. Her parents' protective and secretive powers were not outwardly apparent to young Alice; however, when she turned ten, she became aware that her mother and father were involved in a campaign to rid the world of what they called "Evil doings." The images of a dying planet were unmistakable, and they felt a need to stop the decay.

Alice leaned against the wall. She didn't even know what month or year it was. The entire time cycle started back at one after Blank. She had no frame of reference since her surroundings were just as her parents explained it would be, basic. "You understand the power you hold, don't you?" Atlantis asked Alice. Alice nodded in her head that she supposed so. "But what good is power when you don't know what to do?" This was a question both egos could agree on. What to do? So, they decided to do nothing. Nothing is not actually nothing, Alice pondered. For if it were nothing, there would be a void, which she knew was not possible since she existed. So doing nothing was doing something.

She thought she heard a light rap on the window. It seemed too early for Amazon or Danube. The morning sun had just risen, and the girls were most likely still having breakfast. She got up and went to the window where a pair of hands cupped a face staring inside. It was Nebraska. She wondered what he wanted. "Perhaps it's about Alabama," Atlantis thought and quickly got to her feet, but it was Alice who opened the door. "You're up early," she said; however, after giving him a quick examination, she could tell he had likely not been to sleep.

"Is Danube here?" he asked.

"What's wrong with me?" Alice questioned, feeling excluded. She twisted her head and, like an owl, whipped it back front. "Nope, she's not here." The boy appeared frightened. His eyes glassy and the corners of his mouth quivered. "You look like you've seen a ghost. What's the matter?"

"It's my grandfather," Nebraska said. "I think he's very sick."

"What kind of sick?"

"I don't know, just sick."

"Does he have a fever? Is he throwing up?" Alice was getting a little impatient when Atlantis whispered for her to be more compassionate.

"He's really hot. I put a cool compress on his head, but it doesn't help."

"Did you call a doctor?"

Nebraska nodded yes. "A doctor came by yesterday but said there wasn't anything more she could do. It's his throat. It hurts so bad, and his chest hurts too. I didn't know what to do, so I thought maybe Danube would have some better elixir made from berries."

"Berries!" exclaimed Alice. "Are we making a salad or treating a sick person. Don't worry; I've had that kind of sore throat when I was a kid. It's probably strep." She shook her head woefully and beckoned for him to come inside. "Didn't the doctor give him any medicine like an antibiotic?"

Nebraska's blue eyes narrowed as he pinched his brow. Nothing Alice said made any sense. Yes, he had followed the doctor's directions, but this morning, the old man was not getting any better. His last resort was to find Alabama, which would mean leaving the old man alone. "The doctor told me to give him apple vinegar and honey five times a day."

Alice returned a piercing look. "Yuck! That won't cure strep. You need real medicine." But as she began to chastise him, she realized this was the only remedy available. This was the prescribed treatment in today's world.

"Then what would you do?" Nebraska demanded, daring her to come up with something constructive. His tone was harsh, and instinctively he grew angry. "I'm going back home," he muttered and turned towards the door. His thoughts were muddled as he tried to reconcile how to help his sick grandfather. Nebraska's exhaustion invoked dismay with an overwhelming sense of dread. In the dim light of the morning, he felt miserably vulnerable.

"Do you trust me?" Alice asked the boy. *What are you up to?* Atlantis whispered but was ignored by her alter ego. Nebraska released the door handle and returned to the worktable. "Do you?" Alice asked Nebraska again. She was seriously sincere. "If you don't, then you can wait for Danube and her little sister to come with my breakfast. But I can't imagine they have any more useful help than your doctor offered. Look at these shelves filled with dry seeds."

Nebraska realized the position he was in. He could scarcely take care of himself, let alone his grandfather. The lanky youth leaning over the table was as strange a person he had ever met.

And for the first time, he acknowledged just how unusual. Her sudden arrival in the shed was an enigma, as were her bizarre habits and the way she spoke. But he couldn't think about that now. It didn't matter where she came from. He skimmed over all those non-essential details and got to the point. "Do you? Do you trust this weird girl?" The words rang in his head. "What would Alabama do?" he asked himself.

"Your brother was here before he went away," Atlantis said. *"Why'd you tell him!" whispered Alice.* But this time, Atlantis ignored her alter ego. "Your brother and I are friends. I don't wish to harm you; I just want to help."

"How did you know I was thinking about Alabama?" the perplexed boy asked.

"It just seemed logical. You and I aren't so different. I don't have anyone, and now, neither do you." She repeated the question. "Do you trust me because if you do, I can help." Nebraska followed his intuition and nodded yes. Alice had avoided being caught by the authorities; no one knew who or where she came from. With such cunning, she had no reason to deceive him; none, at least that he could think of.

* * *

When Doc answered the door, she wasn't surprised to see the younger woman standing on the threshold. The sun was streaming in, and the doorway framed her silhouette. "I don't understand how you can wear that jacket in this heat."

"It's my favorite," Dakar Hamlet said. Doc stepped aside and let her inside.

"Who's that?" Dakar asked. She knelt and petted the dog behind the ears.

"My new friend. I call her Cleopatra. Want some coffee, fresh pot on the stove." She led the woman into the kitchen, where Alabama was finishing his toast.

"Good morning," Dakar said, entering the room. She turned to Doc for an explanation. "Isn't he a little young for you?" she smiled and winked.

The boy showed little interest in her off-beat humor and stood up from the table. "Want some coffee?" he asked and took a cup off the shelf. "Milk?" She nodded her head as he poured.

"Mmmm, smells good," Dakar said, signaling approval as he handed her the coffee before she sat down.

"Dakar, this is Alabama, Trenton's grandson. Alabama, this is Dakar, a friend of mine. Alabama will be staying with me for a while." Emphasis placed on the ambiguity of time was understood as having no endpoint. Which, to Dakar, was taken as a probable explanation; the boy was in hiding.

"The sabotage on the bank made quite a stir," Dakar said, taking up the conversation and the necessity for face-to-face contact. "But Rosario's suicide, that has me still wondering, why."

"I'm not convinced she did kill herself," Doc retorted, shutting the burner off under the coffee before sliding the brewed pot aside.

"Then you also think it was murder too?"

"A woman doesn't just end her life over a robbery. Especially when she had nothing to do with it." Dakar shrugged her shoulders. She was satisfied not to extend this probe. People have their reasons, and as far as she was concerned, this was not hers.

Alabama perked up when he heard the word murder. He was a baby wolf learning how to survive. He scrutinized the woman sitting next to him and wanted to trust her. Dakar's ordinary appearance blended in with the other civilians. But she was more than just another civilian. Her botany training earned her a place among the higher-ranking officials in the occupying government's agriculture department: second in charge of the Seed Development and Monetary Unit. Her relationship with Doc began over ten years ago but now continued almost exclusively through encoded messages and an occasional covert rendezvous. She hated the occupiers and, as a member of the cause, considered one of the most valuable agents. "As seemingly mundane as it sounds, the robbery set off major internal alarms. The single most important security weapon against insurrection and foreign enemy takeover is controlling the monetary unit." A tremor of a smile appeared on Dakar's lips after she spoke while having directed this explanation as if thinking aloud.

But this was all new to the boy, and his quiet personality sought more. "Could there be others?" he asked naively.

"We made many more attempts a decade ago," Doc interjected. "But some of our partners grew complacent over the years and eventually less and less involved. Some are in prison, others sent to labor camps, or simply missing." The woman placed her hand on his shoulder and squeezed gently. "Listen carefully, young-blood, and learn about noble sedition. Right now, the occupiers control the entire global seed currency market. It's illegal to hoard or trade seeds that are not government-issued. The occupiers have the entire economy tied to their banks. But, by integrating heritage seeds, referred to on the black market as open-pollinated varieties, we might be able to disrupt and weaken their financial control. Why do you think there are so many gathers? They need you."

Alabama rearranged the information, sorting such implications to his narrow life. "What does that mean?" he asked.

"It means our covert objective is to bring the forces of competition into the currency markets and diminish the total power of the central banks. Citizens should be free to use any currency of their choosing, even if that means enforcing the rejection of the chosen one." Doc continued to fill the sugar bowl as she spoke. Alabama thought this was an odd thing to be doing while talking about something so important. Nevertheless, he envied her self-assurance and cavalier attitude. "What news do you have?" she asked, turning to her friend. Doc placed the sugar canister back on the shelf and sat down at the table, stirring her coffee aimlessly. Dakar tossed a questioning glance towards the boy. "He's fine," Doc assured him. "Besides, it's obvious he knows too much after our speeches. Plus, if he leaves, he'll be picked up."

Alabama shrank back into his chair, feeling like a delinquent. "Okay, then," Dakar said, her face becoming curiously expressionless. She folded her hands and leaned in. "I intercepted a memo regarding a new arrival. It seems that night surveillance teams have confirmed a pretty good chance of entrance near or around this area."

"Pretty good chance?" Doc asked with little conviction. However, with the mention of a newcomer, she immediately thought about the exchange made by the girls. It was a blanket for a friend.

"Well, no one can be sure, and unless a district team goes on a massive search, the only thing we can go on is pretty good. I imagine for a bag of sesame seeds, I might be able to get more information, but I think that would put my cover at risk."

Doc nodded her head in agreement. "And, if this information is correct?" she added, remaining passively neutral.

"The safest thing to do is to find the newcomer and turn them in, securing our position as loyalists." She finished her coffee and lifted the cup for a refill. "I never could stop at one," she laughed.

The minutes that had passed prolonged the boy's silent agitation. Things were moving too fast and too strangely. The sun rose today, but it was not on its daily course; the red dawn had spread unevenly. Alabama wished to distill the information into a few words, a simple answer, but that was impossible. All his rearranging came up with the same fact. A hunted newcomer, if caught, would be sacrificed for "the cause." Alabama's eyes widened with anticipation, aware of his unintentional involvement, aware of the consequences, and suddenly aware of who the newcomer could be.

Chapter 15

Deputy Khanna was unofficially reprimanded for "failure to carry out a duty in an effective amount of time." This put him in a very unpleasant mood when he arrived at work. He was particularly surly to Deputy Gris, who tried to appease his superior with a cup of coffee. However, the tepid beverage only added fuel to his already bad disposition. Both men were now gloomy, and no amount of coffee or pleasantries could fix the situation. Khanna had hoped for a promotion taking him out of his office under the guard post and into a more prestigious position. He wished to work in the administrative offices where lunch could be served in the cafeteria and coffee made by a real cook. Instead, he turned and scowled at Gris, muttering something indiscernible under his breath. "What?" the bystander asked.

"It's your coffee; it's always lousy." Gris looked down at his cup like a chastised dog and said nothing. "Did the morning review arrive yet?" Khanna asked the dejected man. However, he didn't need to ask since the morning report with today's date was lying in the open folder in front of him, June 4. "I assume you took time to review it?" Khanna hated wading through government memos filled with information he didn't care about or unrelated to his cases.

"The usual stuff. A few minor infractions, illegal settlements broken up, you know."

"No, I don't know; otherwise, I wouldn't be asking you." Khanna raised his eyes to the Deputy in disgust and handed him the folder.

Gris opened it up and skimmed the pages. There was a total of 16, all of which he only had looked at with a casual eye earlier. His finger ran up and down the margin until page 10, where he stopped reading. "A newcomer," he announced. He handed the page back to Khanna. The Senior Deputy read the information slowly as if chewing each word. He set the page down and laughed aloud.

* * *

The old man's bedroom had large beams running lengthwise across the ceiling. He never took any notice of the cobwebs, probably because he never spent much time staring up. It was dark, and he wasn't sure what time of the day it was. He felt overpowered by weakness, but with Nebraska's help, he leaned up against the pillow. In the boy's outstretched palm was a small oblong object. He studied it for a moment before speaking.

"Swallow it with water," Nebraska said. A tin cup was waiting on the nightstand.

"What is it?" He was burning up with fever.

Nebraska didn't know. "It's going to help you get better."

"That?" The incredulous tone made even Nebraska smile. "Where'd you get that?"

But Nebraska was not so sure he should discuss his recent outing. Even if he told him that a strange girl hiding in the shed gave him a dozen of these pills, he wouldn't believe it. "Trust me, grandpa, it will make you get better. Nothing else has."

"You want me to swallow this?" he picked up the pill with great suspicion. "The last time I did something like this was when your grandmother dared me to eat a snail. She said it was French. I don't suppose this will taste as good." Nebraska offered the water, and the old man did as asked. "Now what?" he asked slyly. Nebraska gently moved the pillow so his grandfather could lie back down. The boy dipped the compress in cold water and placed it on the fevered forehead. "You're not really a good-for-nothing," the elder whispered. "You're a good boy, Nebraska. A good boy."

Nebraska sat and wondered if he had done the right thing. Alice said he would be feeling better after all the pills were taken two times a day with water. He reached into his pocket and laid the small bundle on the nightstand. Now all he had to do was wait. He peered over the sleeping man and removed the damp cloth. He dipped it into the water and wrung it out. But when he tried to place it on the forehead, he was stopped by the old man's hand reaching up. "No more. I just need to rest." The young guardian abandoned his post and tiptoed out of the room. He walked down the stairs and found the dog sitting by the front door.

"You miss Grampa, don't you," he said. Then he opened the door to let the dog out. A sweet smell of sunshine entered, but the boy felt as if the entire world had turned to pitch. The sleeping man upstairs had become mortal, and that frightened him.

* * *

"Haunted by a wish. It is exhausting. Maybe that's why I'm tired," Alice thought. She had put on the drab muslin tunic, her feet were bare, and the shower curtain pulled over her shoulders. Dressed like this, she felt like Alice and not the look-alike Atlantis. There were some things Atlantis still didn't know, and this notion made her wish again. But she was sworn to secrecy. *When you wake up, you will see how different you are from everyone else. If you try to explain where you came from, I am sure no one will believe you. If anything goes wrong, use what we have taught you as a guide. Don't be afraid; you can outwit them all. You must promise not to tell too much; it won't be safe.* Now she understood what her mother meant. Something had gone wrong; she was alone. Then why wasn't she scared? *"Because I'm with you,"* whispered Atlantis. *"No,"* said Alice. *"It's because we understand each other. My perception of you as not me makes me who I am, and your perception of me as not you makes you who you are."*

It was a great burden knowing so much and knowing so little. It was like wearing one blue sock and one black sock. Which one is correct? Together they cancel each other out;

individually, they are waiting for the other mate, which makes them not a whole pair or incomplete. And then it dawned on her she might be the only person who was not incomplete. She lived on both sides of Blank. *You must promise not to tell too much; it won't be safe.* She had emerged from the void unseen, unheard, and in total anonymity.

The day was slowly coming to life, and the soft hours of the morning with their pale blue shadows. She tried to remember the dream that had woken her up. The hut was on fire, and the doorway blocked by flames licking the walls. At the moment the blaze leaped into the room, a mockingbird outside the widow spoke to her. "Follow me." She turned to the window and tried to pull it open, but it was stuck. It took several tries until it released itself. A cool breeze entered and at once began to fan the flames until they were out. Then the mockingbird spoke again. "Bury me." It was a curious thing to say until she realized the bird had swallowed the fire to save her. Alice smiled. *Such an unselfish thing for the mockingbird to do. I will remember that.*

* * *

Word spread quickly, with whispers and rumors circulating in the region. The old man, on his death bed, miraculously recovered. For a week, the doctor said his condition was hopeless, and the only care he received was the constant presence of his grandson tending to his needs and an herbal serum the doctor prescribed. It wasn't until a probe by the regional health department did a suspicious event come out. Aside from the routinely prescribed tincture, Old Man Bailiwick was swallowing chalk-like pills, no bigger than a piece of gravel. According to their inquiry, he was fully cured after five days, as if nothing had ever ailed him. Clearly, it wasn't the boy who healed him, but instead, someone or something else. The chance to shine a light on the matter was through the old man or the boy. There was every reason to believe Nebraska was withholding knowledge of witchcraft.

"Witchcraft!" laughed Atlantis, hearing the news. "You can't be serious!" But neither Danube nor Amazon found her remarks as funny. "You're not fooling!" said Atlantis. "They really think there's a witch."

"Are you?" asked Amazon as if she hoped the intruder might just be one.

"Of course, she's not!" scolded Danube. "If she were, she wouldn't be hiding in here."

"I'm not hiding," repeated Atlantis. "I'm residing." She smiled and resumed sorting sunflower seeds into piles of ten. The sisters had given up trying to prevent the intruder from playing with the jars. It was decided that as long as she didn't eat the seeds, it would be alright. "Breakfast, I presume," remarked Atlantis. She pushed the piles aside, opened the brown bag, and pulled out a folded slice of bread. Immediately she began to consume the contents. Danube and Amazon watched as the youth finished the meager sandwich they had brought. She wiped her mouth on the back of her hand and smiled. "Anything else?" she asked.

"How can you be hungry after what Nebraska told us what you did. It was very nice of you to help, but now, I'm afraid you must leave." Danube stood with her hand on her hip, impatiently tapping her foot.

"You look like Mother!" Amazon squealed.

"Oh, shut up, Amazon! Can't you see this is a problem? A big problem."

"The world is a big place, and I am sure you and your family will find a suitable place to live. As for myself, I have no reason to leave. However, if you find my presence a nuisance, then I suggest you go at once," Alice answered.

"But if you're found they'll say you're a witch!" Daube said.

"And if they don't find me, I won't be a witch. So, I had better stay put. Besides, I don't want to change my brand again. I really would like to go back to my original name. I can't imagine what name I would be given if I were a witch."

"She's right, Danube," agreed Amazon.

The girls, as usual, were perplexed by Alice. Danube hesitated and simply sighed. "But Mother is bound to start snooping around. You know how things frighten her, especially with Father away on the frontier. So she pretends to be strong."

"My mother is very strong," Alice said. "But I can't speak for Atlantis; I really don't think we have the same mother."

"Then you'll have to stay," replied the younger sister. She had grown to like the strange girl, and the idea of her departure made her sad. "Danube, where would Alice go? If she leaves, she'll certainly get caught. She's better here with us where we can feed her."

"She's not a stray dog, for heaven's sake!" exclaimed the older girl.

"No, but she is our friend, and she did save Mr. Bailiwick from dying!" said Amazon. Atlantis's mouth, full of the bread, stopped chewing. Her eyes grew wide, and then she swallowed. Her silent smile awaited Danube's response to the younger, wiser sister.

"Then, we will need to keep this shed off-limits from anyone entering. But for how long?" Danube thought aloud. There was an enormous hole in her mental plan. Only a wall could keep trespassers out. It would be tall and ominous, terrifying enough to prevent the occupiers from scaling and getting over. But this grand barrier only lived in her head; there was no wall or moat or alligator pit. "Deputy Gris was at our house," Danube exclaimed. "He instructed mother to be on the lookout for any suspicious person wandering around. If she does or finds out anything, she's to report the information directly to him. That's why you're in danger of being found out. The occupiers are going door-to-door alerting people."

"It seems that Deputy Gris is always hunting for someone. Isn't he looking for Alabama too? He has a bad habit of losing people," Alice remarked, noting she was not the least bit concerned. "I don't think he's very good at his job; by now, he should have made some progress. Although I admit my parents are misplaced, although I expect their arrival within the next decade."

"In ten years!" despaired Danube.

"Maybe less. It was careless of my parents to miss their opportunity to arrive with me. But I have great faith they'll be delivered eventually. You see, that's why I can't leave." Atlantis surrendered back inside the ego, giving Alice full reign of the conversation. It was Alice who was the scaffold of their stability, and without intent, displayed a power beyond anyone's ability. And although some thought the power was evil, others believed her power might be quite the opposite. So, it would quickly come to pass that those in the region would set out to find the possessed for different reasons.

* * *

"Who gave you the tablets?" demanded the old man.

Nebraska, who had been snipping off the dried heads of dandelions, suddenly felt the grandfather's presence. "Tablets?"

"They're going to take you in if you don't tell me." He observed his grandson by way of these plain facts. Nebraska set the clippers in his back pocket and wiped his face on his sleeve. It was hot in the garden, and the question only exacerbated his discomfort. He knew he couldn't lie, but to tell the truth would put everyone at risk. He furrowed his brow.

The old man could read the boy's expression. "If it was a newcomer, then you need to tell me."

"I don't know; she didn't say where she was from."

"So, it was a she. An old she or a young she."

"Young. But we can't tell anyone!" A moment of guilt scolded the boy. "Promise me, Grandpa. Promise me, swear you won't tell."

"I'm not tellin' anyone anything. There's nothing to tell. As far as I know, you got them from a traveler passing through. You got that Nebraska, an old veteran traveling through our region. He had no papers and was in a wagon. No, not a wagon, walking. Okay, an old veteran walking. A stranger came to the door. He asked you for water. You told him about me, and he sold you the tablets in exchange for seeds."

"What kind of seeds?" Nebraska asked.

"Chervil, a whole damn bag of chervil for the tablets." The old man was perspiring and leaned wearily against the fence. "Now tell me what I said."

"An old veteran came to the house asking for water. When he asked if I was alone, I told him you were sick, and I paid him a bag of seeds for the tablets."

"Chervil, boy, remember chervil seeds. They'll ask you to describe the man. Just say you don't remember."

"I don't remember because I was too worried about my grandfather," Nebraska added.

"Good, that's good." Trenton Bailiwick had grown weary. He thought about the firearm he had stored in the attic. The pistol wasn't fired since the failed insurrection. He had buried the ammunition and hoped he could get more if needed. He would not hide both his grandson's. Alabama could take care of himself, but Nebraska, he was still just a kid. The hound followed the old man on the hard trodden path back to the house. The old man carried the hickory stick he had cut and sanded. Strangely he found himself smiling, an expression he rarely did, and that made him wonder if he had forgotten something. *Maybe I'm smiling because I'm not dead.* The boy saved his life, and he never thanked him or the mysterious she with the tablets. Instead, he took comfort in the house that appeared before him. He raised the stick and rested it on his shoulder. "That you, Mrs. Pacific?" A small middle-aged woman emerged from behind the house and was hurrying towards him.

"Yes, it's me, Trenton!" She stopped and waited for him by the steps. "I heard about you; in fact, everyone knows what happened." Her voice raised an octave with worry. The old man nodded his head and slowly walked up the steps to the porch. "We heard you were dying!" She stood behind him as he opened the door and followed him into the foyer.

"Not quite dead, as you can see, I'm alive." He laughed and patted his arms and legs.

"You know what I mean," the woman exclaimed. "I don't know if it's black magic, but I need to find out who cured you. There's been some wicked things going on."

"What kind of wicked things?" The old man offered her a chair, but she was too anxious to sit.

"Your grandson, he could take me there," she suggested. "Which one is it, the younger? Nebraska?"

"Take you where, Mrs. Pacific?"

"To the witch, take me to the witch."

"What witch, who said anything about a witch?"

"Deputy Gris, he came around and said anyone that could lead him to the witch would get a reward. And I began to think, you and your grandson must know. So if you just tell Nebraska to show me the way, I won't implicate you. No, not at all."

"Implicate?"

"Why yes, it only seems logical that you must know the witch. We understand your reluctance to turn it in. But," she paused and stopped pacing, "if you lead me to her, she'll never know it was you or your grandson. Why my husband and I will share the reward with you!" She had already made her point and had no intention of recounting her decision. "If you choose not to help, I am sure the location will be found out anyway."

"What makes you think this person is evil? Perhaps it is just a good person with no intention of doing harm."

"The officials, they told us."

"And you're going to take the word of the officials, the occupiers?"

"I am afraid we have no choice," the woman claimed. "If it isn't me then it will be someone else."

"And what if I told you that the tablets I took were bought from a veteran passing through the region."

"A veteran? One of ours?" Mrs. Pacific asked.

The old man nodded his head and sighed. "I can't be sure because I didn't see him. But I can assure you; he was not a witch, just a simple man on his way passing through the region. It was weeks ago, so he must be in the frontier by now. If you and your husband want to find him, go out there."

A look of disappointment crossed her face. "So, there was no witch." She muttered. Her demeanor relaxed, and she sat down in the chair and placed her pocketbook on her lap.

"No, Mrs. Pacific, no witch. Just a poor man. Just one of us." He almost felt sorry for the neighbor but at the same time annoyed. He looked at the clock; time had stood still, and though it was only a few minutes since her arrival, the old man did not want Nebraska to come in while she was still in the house. "Well, if there is nothing else I can do?" his voice wandered, allowing her to take the cue.

"No, I suppose not." Doubt lingered from her words as she stood up and allowed the old man to usher her to the door. "I am glad you're not dead," she giggled.

"Me too." He did not giggle; he was dead serious.

Mrs. Pacific stepped out onto the porch where the hound had coiled up in the corner. "You do know; there will be others."

"Others?" Bailiwick remarked, feigning not to understand.

"Other folks are wanting information about the witch."

The old man shrugged. "I know you will set them straight and tell them otherwise," he answered.

"Naturally, Trenton. Isn't that what good neighbors are for?" She rearranged her handbag over her arm and, holding the railing, stepped down onto the dirt path, lightly treading as if she were walking on glass.

"My best to your Mr.," he called. But she didn't hear him as she fell out of sight down the gravel road.

Chapter 16

I *am, and I was.* Alice thought about this statement. *I am not only my future, but I am my past.* This too, she contemplated. *The present is stagnant until I make a choice. But my choice is stagnant because I have no alternative approach to the mess I have found the world in.* She turned her attention to Atlantis, who had little understanding of this train of thought. *It would be nice if you could give me some of your ideas about what to do.* "Me," whispered the alter ego. "I don't know; I'm just here to fill in until you get your whole self back again." Alice closed her eyes and pondered. Atlantis was right, but she did have an obligation to give some advice; otherwise, *she would have to just get rid of her.* "I heard that!" exclaimed Atlantis. "If you want to know, I think you should leave me behind and get out." *Leave you behind? Alice remarked. And what would happen to you?* "I'll just hang around, and if you need me, then you can easily conjure me up again." But leaving didn't feel right. She was strangely content in this shed. It was her shed, just at a different time. *My existence is the past, a self-illusion no one else could relate to, except for Atlantis.*

We'll stay here for a little longer; she told Atlantis. Just a bit more time. "Tell me again about the mole," Atlantis asked. Alice leaned against the wall and tucked the shower curtain around them both. *It was a little rhyme my parents used to recite, a funny little saying. If things got tough, follow the mole.* "Then I think it's a grand time to recite it to me too," Atlantis suggested.

Along the lonely countryside
Golden wheat grows shoulder high
Where Mr. Mole makes fairy rings
And up above the blackbirds sing
He burrows tunnels all around
Building homes beneath the ground
His favorite game is hide and seek
Find him at the old mill creek
Travel at an easy pace
Until the stones are out of place
Look to the east and down split logs
Part the reeds to see the frogs
Follow the mole where the old creek falls
And red vines climb over stony-walls

There, what do you think? Alice asked after the recitation. "I think your parents were very wise," replied the alter- ego. *Perhaps, thought Alice.*

＊ ＊ ＊

Mrs. Rivers revisited the recent conversation with Senior Deputy Khanna. She was surprised at how cordial he was. A man of his ranking asked if she wanted coffee, if she took it black or with cream and sugar. He was not what she expected, but then, she had never before been summoned to the Regional Office. The questions were reasonable, she decided. The authority's interest in the incident with the Bailiwicks was for her own good and the neighbor's. Perhaps her adding that she didn't like Trenton Bailiwick wasn't such a smart thing to divulge. Saying that he was too, too...? She couldn't come up with the words.

"Secretive?" the Deputy asked. Yes, secretive. But now, in her own living room, she wondered if that was the word she meant. Secretive, she rolled the word over in her mouth like a marble. But it didn't matter. She answered the questions honestly and without hesitation. There was only one thing she neglected to mention when asked if she had any idea where the witch could hide. She had forgotten all about the garden shed. She'd look there by herself when the girls were in bed. The garden shed might just be a space to conceal someone. Why, she might be entitled to a considerable reward if her hunch was correct. Khanna said he would help her if she helped him. Such a grand idea suited the mother well, and she smiled cunningly to herself.

* * *

Less than an hour after the children were asleep, Mrs. Rivers went out the backdoor. The moon was low, it was a cloudless night, and the only item she carried was a kitchen knife. She pointed the blade in front of her as she walked, slowly following the path to the shed. The bushes framing the way needed pruning; their long tendrils leaned in all directions tickling her ankles. More than once did she swat away a spider web, making her wonder if her nighttime investigation warranted reason to turn back. So many wild ideas were going through her head. What would she really do if she did find someone in the shed? The knife wavered in her hand, and she felt herself clutching the handle as if it were a dagger and not a bread knife.

The shed was directly in front of the mother as she walked ever so slowly to the door. It looked less run down in the moonlight; however, she remembered how much work needed to be done as she clasped the doorknob in her hand. She had assumed the witch inside was a woman, but suddenly it occurred that it might indeed be a man. A warlock! A steely shaft of fright ran up her spine as she shivered, not with cold but with fear. The knob turned quickly as she quietly pushed the door open. A slight creak sounded, startling the mother by her action. She slipped the knife through first, keeping it parallel to the floor with the blade leading. Her eyes tried to adjust to the gloom. Her hand reached forward as her feet followed. A moonbeam offered some reprieve from the darkness through the window. She set the knife down and stood silently, listening for any sign of life. She rounded the table. A shower curtain bundled in the corner appeared to be tossed over something. But it was not that which attracted attention. Her glance at the shelves demanded more scrutiny. She had an excellent eye for detail, and even in the dimness of the shed, she could tell that there was something amiss. "Damn!" she exclaimed. "Damn, damn, damn!" The seeds that took years of collecting had been tampered with. The jars were out of order and definitely not in rows. She lifted the sunflower seeds and brought the jar to her face. Then she set it back and took another jar from the shelf, flax. Then the beans and pumpkin. All had been tampered with; stolen! The witch robbed them! Her mind erupted with anger as she shoved the jars away from the ledge. Her head throbbed. She looked at the knife in the moonlight, and it gave her a power she was suddenly afraid of.

"What a fool I was to store the seeds in the shed," Mrs. Rivers muttered. She went over to the window and tried to pull it open, but years of neglect kept it forever stuck closed. "Good," she thought. She pulled out a step from under the worktable, placing it by the shelf. She stood on it and ran her hand over the top shelf, locating the padlock and key. Dust floated down over her head, extending her disgust. "Tomorrow, I'll go back to the Deputy and report the theft," she decided. Shoving the step back beneath the table, she picked up the knife. "No, I can't," she suddenly realized. "I can't tell them." It occurred to her that they would believe she had been harboring the witch. They would accuse her of conspiring. Her hands began to tremble; her focus lost to indecision. Weighed down with the burden of untamed thoughts, she removed a bucket from the bottom shelf and quickly filled it with seed jars. She placed it outside the door and paused in the doorway. A sense of relief drew up through her breath, and she exhaled long and hard. But her sense of respite was premature.

A silent conviction pressed her forward. She removed a jar of matches stored on the shelf and grabbed a handful of dried hay. She sensed an uneasiness in the shed as if someone was watching. "The witch!" she thought. "Its specter is here!" Finally, the terrified woman found her courage and lit the wooden match; she held the blue flame to the chaff. Like lightning striking prairie grass, the straw ignited with a vengeance. Mrs. Rivers stood in the open doorway as the fire crawled up the table leg. A twist of black smoke rose, filling the garden hut with hazy grey plumes. Her wishes were being carried out more suddenly than she anticipated. "Depart from here, you devilish witch!" she cried. A suppressed excitement inside of her spilled out as the wooden table collapsed, shattering into kindling. Then in a matter of seconds, an explosion shook the building, knocking the mother off her feet. The garden shed was entombed in a fury of flames, and the smell of turpentine depleted all fresh air. It was not a challenge for the fire. Licks of flames reached the rafters and began to scar the roof in black soot before scorching the wood. Its only salvation may have been the open door and a windless night. In what may account to be only minutes since the inception of the hideous crime, the quiet moonlit path transformed into a chaotic and desperate scene. The dangerous and daunting job of trying to extinguish the fire did not deter the sisters. Blue flames pressed against the window creating a death trap exit.

As if it were a candle, only the rooftop was burning so vehemently. "We have to put it out!" screamed Amazon. "We have to get to the pump!" Danube followed the younger girl around to the back. The fire heckled ferociously, making her tremble. "Maybe she got out!" cried Amazon. "Maybe she's okay!"

But Danube did not answer. She was too afraid of what she was thinking. Her hands were shaking, and she could barely pump the handle. "It's stuck!"

"It can't be!" squealed Amazon. "Let me help!" In the dark of the night, everything felt wrong. Stepping forward, she kicked the tin bucket, and its clamor sent the two girls into a frantic cry of fright. Realizing it was only the bucket, Amazon repositioned it under the spout, and they both tried again, this time with success. Water splashed their bare feet and dampened their nightgowns, but they didn't care; they tried again. Once more, they pushed up and down, and the old pump filled water to the brim. But before they tried to lift the pail, they heard a voice calling out to them.

"Come away, come away from there!" a cry of anguish rose louder than the burning shed. Reeling from faintness, Mrs. Rivers appeared like a phantom. Her breath came quick and fitful. "Did you girls hear me?" Her nightmarish image claimed their worst imaginations, and when she approached, Danube lurched back. It wasn't until the protest of voices hollering above the commotion of a pealing bell, did both girls become aware of the presence of the fire brigade. A fire engine tore into the yard, its steam rising like a furnace. Half a dozen men established "fire lines" near the burning building. Chief Krakow had assumed command, and the firefighters worked swiftly under his orders. Directly ahead of them was a trail of smoke and red cinders. The length of the black hose was curling and thrashing about the ground like a great sea snake. The contents of the building were so flammable that the water thrown upon it carried out little effect. The windowpanes had blown out in the explosion during which the triumphant fire took down the roof, yet the searing door remained.

"You girls, move back! Move back!"

Despite their frantic pleas, Mrs. River's heeded the demand and pulled her children away. "We have to find her!" cried Amazon. "We need to find her!"

"Her, her?" questioned the mother. "It's a witch, and now it's gone! It burned in the fire, gone for good! Look!" she exclaimed. Then, holding her children close to her side, she whipped them around to witness the devastation. The roofless shed had never gained so much attention. The four walls charred by fire were saturated with water. The children whimpered like puppies. Cold and exhausted, they clung to their mother. "Everything will be alright now," whispered Mrs. Rivers.

"How can it be," cried Amazon. "She's in there. Look, no one could get out!" That she wouldn't see the strange girl again made her bury her face in her hands.

"It's all our fault," confessed Danube. "If only we could have got here sooner."

Clouds of grey smoke rose above the victorious firefighters. They had overpowered their enemy and now turned their attention to the surrounding area.

"The garden will never be the same," muttered Mrs. Rivers as she watched the flooding of her paltry vegetable plot.

Chief Krakow calmly approached the quivering woman and her children. An unsettled drooping of his eyes tried to sympathize. If he could only muster a tint of compassion. But he was not a compassionate man. So, he offered the next best thing, the truth. "You're a lucky woman. Had there been just an inkling of wind, this fire could have jumped the stone path and spread up to the house. As it is, you've got a mess." He pointed to the burned garden shed and scorched brush. "At least the outhouse wasn't touched. We got here in time." Mrs. Rivers greeted that news with a sigh of relief. "And," Chief Krakow added, patting each girl on the head, "which one of you quick thinkers had the smarts to call us?"

"Call you?" asked Danube. "It couldn't have been one of us." She surveyed the tall man deciding he was an oaf.

"We don't have a phone," said Amazon.

Mrs. Rivers remained silent, appearing as confused as Krakow. "Well, someone called, and it was a girl with a strange name. It sounded like Atlanta," he said.

"Could it have been Atlantis?" Danube asked.

"Yes, I believe that is what she said. Atlantis."

Chapter 17

Dear Amazon and Danube,

Days passed as if on wings since I arrived and filled up all the empty spaces. But now that there is no more garden shed, I am leaving. Even if your mother hadn't set fire to it, I couldn't stay there indefinitely since I would have outgrown my clothes. Atlantis is staying behind because she is fragile. She has neither substance, form, shape, voice, or anything that can provide her presence. She is also naive and accepts your world, although she will not submit to it. As for me, my relationship with your place in history is a metaphor. But to avoid its existence would be to accept finality, and I'm not ready for that.

My past is your future which makes my nostalgia not very unique. So, here I am, free to move on and will leave the way I arrived. Don't worry about me. I am equipped to find my way forward and, by following the mole, am free as the clouds. I have a surprise for you both, but you will have to be patient. Thanks for the hospitality.

Your friend,

Alice

It was Danube who first discovered the note stuck under the bedroom door. The dress they had given Alice was balled up and set aside in the corner of the hallway. Each sister took a turn reading the note, and then Danube read it aloud. After some discussion, they decided they didn't understand a single word.

* * *

It was Alabama who discovered the dog's real name stamped on the underside of the red collar. "She's Inja."

"Inja, you don't say. No wonder she never comes when I call her," Doc complained. "Finally, I can rest knowing why she always ignores me. Well, Inja, it's a good thing because I was beginning to think you didn't like me," the woman exclaimed, pulling the canine by the collar. "You've done a good job keeping her coat brushed. I don't suppose you found out where she was from."

Alabama smiled. "No, I'm afraid she's here to stay." The dog looked at its companion as if having something to say. She would have much to relay if she could speak, but being as dogs can't, she was satisfied to remain silent. "I'll take her out back; we both need to stretch our legs."

Breakfast was over and the morning dishes piled up in the sink; not enough hot water to wash them. Hamlet was sitting on the back porch finishing her coffee when a knock fell on the door. She heard Doc open it, and a muffled conversation began. Finally, the door closed, and the old man followed the invitation into the kitchen and sat down. "Coffee?"

He nodded yes and sat back wearily, setting his cap on the table. "I better let the boy know what's going on," he said. He looked briefly around as if waiting for an apparition to appear. He felt obliged to make excuses for his gaunt appearance as if he needed to explain away the drabness he felt in this well-lit kitchen. But Doc appeared not to notice, ignoring the chatter in his head.

"He's out back with the dog. I got tired of waiting for your hound, so I bought myself a dog."

Trenton smiled. "That's okay; I gave the little ones away; they were eating me out of the house. One dog is enough." He tossed a glance at the jacket flung over the chair. "Company?"

"You remember Dakar Hamlet," she motioned to the porch.

"She only comes around when there's good news or bad news."

"Is there any other kind?" Doc laughed. Her voice faded into inquiry. "So, you think that's the end of the newcomer?"

"Let's just say Mrs. Rivers took care of any doubts. But I need to let Alabama know. He's friends with her girls."

"You believe the story?"

"Not any more than you do. But it's best to let the entire event go. If the authorities think the newcomer was a witch, who are we to dispute. And," he continued, "if they think she, or he, is dead, let sleeping dogs lie." He peered up over his coffee and took a slurp.

The old man mistrusted the world as much as Doc. Somehow everything ended with drama. "What will you tell Alabama?"

"Same thing I'm telling you."

Doc sat down and put her finger up to her lips, gesturing a secret. The old man leaned his head forward. "Nothing about your suspicions to Dakar," she whispered. "When you talk to Alabama, take him out alone." Trenton countered her with questioning eyes. "She's different, more radical; kind of how we were at that age."

The old man pulled back and grimaced. "Should I move Alabama?" Suddenly this out-of-the-way haven seemed not so safe.

"She's leaving. Besides, where would he go?" she announced, recounting the trouble the boy was in. "You want me to call him in?"

The old man stood up and stretched. "I don't want to be called lazy," he said. "No, I'll go out and talk with him. But then, I better get back home. Got Nebraska snipping off dried heads from the stalks. I got behind on my quota when I was sick. Not everyone's self-sufficient." He smiled slyly and sauntered off.

Daker watched from the window the reunion between grandfather and grandson. It was a bond she would never understand. "Did I miss anything?" The woman's curiosity was forever probing.

Doc walked over to where she was standing and pulled back the curtain. "No, Trenton just misses having him at home, I suppose."

The answer did not come with any sentimental attachment for Dakar. "This is a nice room," she said, changing the subject. "You're lucky. Not many people have a room like this. It's a porch with windows. Very functional."

"You sound almost domesticated," Doc said. "That scares me."

"Domesticated, bite your tongue!" Dakar yowled. "The day I get domesticated, we might just as well say it's the end!" Both women looked at each other and laughed. "Ironic, isn't it? We only laugh at catastrophes."

"Some would say it's a safety valve. Like when people laugh at a funeral; a way of coping."

Dakar nodded her head in agreement. "What's Trenton really here for besides playing grandpa?"

"To let me know there was a fire, and the newcomer won't be a problem to anyone."

"Which means?"

"We can go about our business without interference." Doc hoped this was the end of the discussion. She was feeling uncomfortable with Dakar, and she wished her guest would leave.

The younger woman pulled a pad from her pocket and flipped the pages. "We never talked about the big nine."

"That's what infiltration is all about. Disseminate black market heritage seeds to combat genetic uniformity. What else didn't we discuss? The big nine will eventually no longer pose a problem if we can boost limited varieties." Doc continued to keep her eye on the man and boy outside.

"Then there's the sticky problem of counter-seed piracy."

"That's always been around," Doc said, waving her hand nonchalantly.

"Maybe, but it's beginning to overstep our small but steady progress. Which goes back to the newcomer," Dakar said. The harshness in her voice showed disdain for the unknown person of question.

Doc tossed the window curtain aside and turned toward her guest. "Now I'm confused."

"If the newcomer makes local contacts, it's more than likely their only means of trading unwittingly, or maybe wittingly, will be with the seed currency they brought with them. In which case, such infiltration could easily corrupt our efforts once theirs gets into the general population. That's why I want to know how you're so sure about this fire?"

"I have no reason to doubt the news Trenton brought me isn't true."

"And the newcomer, were they the arsonist or the victim?"

"We have nothing to fear," Doc reassured her friend. Her eyes met the younger woman like a fiery lantern.

"Then the arsonist is owed a bit of gratitude. Having rid the ignorant populous of a witch and giving us a plausible cover, we have less to worry about."

The two sat on the porch staring out the window. But, as they sat, gossip about the witch ran amuck. Fabricated stories concluded under grave suspicion alleging the River sisters may have engaged in magic arts.

"What!" proclaimed Alabama. His passionate exclaim took on the primary role of protester. "Why didn't Nebraska come and get me?"

"You know damn well why," the old man claimed. "Besides, he did good. Yes, he did. He might be the young one, but don't underestimate your brother." They walked about aimlessly as the old man finished his tale. He explained about the illness, the white pills, and the strange girl he had never met. Then he concluded with the fire. Inja trailed them to the well. The old man reached into his pocket and tossed a pebble into the opening.

"What'd you do that for?" Alabama exclaimed.

"Before our time, people used to toss coins into wells for good luck. Then they'd make a wish. Kind of like paying for something good to happen. Except, the only thing of value in my pocket was my lucky stone."

The boy searched the man's face for understanding. "You don't mean you threw in your..."

"I did," Trenton interrupted. "It seemed the time was right to make a wish."

"You, grandpa, made a wish?" he smiled with disbelief. "What'd you wish for?"

The old man looked squarely into the questioning face of his grandson. "Now, if I told you, my wish wouldn't come true, would it."

"Guess not," Alabama agreed. He knew what he would wish if he had something of value to toss in. But he didn't, so he'd have to go on trusting his instincts. For several quiet moments, they stared into the cavernous opening. "I can't stay here; you know that." *I can't stay here; you know that.*

"Which one can't, you or the echo?" Trenton asked.

Alabama lifted his head and turned. "I have to find the girl who helped you. Her name is Alice, but you can't tell a soul. Swear to me, you won't tell."

"I already did all the promise swearing to your brother. Once is enough for you boys," the old man grumped. "What makes you so sure you'll find her? And if you do, then what? You got a plan, cause if you don't, you damn well better come up with a plan. There's a woman inside Doc's house who's determined to do right, even if it's at the expense of others. Doing righteous does not preclude doing evil." Calm was forfeited, and the old man could see he no longer had a hold on the boy. For over fifty years he secluded himself in secrecy and today offered up a wish into the abyss. Life may be given in many ways, and in his old patient sublime manner, victory condescends while his wise years are muffled by time.

Inja ignored the man and the boy, following her heroic instincts to keep them safe from any marauding animals. She poked her nose anywhere it would fit, causing herself unnecessary sneezing. "I have a sort of idea," Alabama said.

"A sort of idea isn't good enough. Mountains can't be moved with good intentions, nor can intentions arrive without plans." They were both weary, and it was apparent no more needed to be added. "Would you be willing to share this with Doc?"

Doubt assailed Alabama before he answered. "Maybe," he finally said. "If you think it could help."

* * *

Doc would wait for the old man and the boy to come back into the house before returning to the kitchen. She waited with impatience for her friend to finally draw away from the window when Dakar turned her eyes on her hostess. "You know," she said, "I don't really think I have ever looked at you." She smiled and, like a bird, cocked her head to the side. "Come closer; what color are your eyes?"

"Green," Doc said. "What color are yours?"

"Blue." Dakar walked away from the window and stood beside Doc's chair. She knelt and stared into her friend's eyes. "No, I think they're hazel."

"Hazel?"

"Yes," she pointed up to Doc's face. "There, I can see a few specks of brown."

"No, they've always been green."

"Well, not today. I tell you, I see brown."

Doc shrugged her shoulder and laughed. "Well, if you say so, but I am not budging, my eyes are green." It was a rather strange conversation, trivial in nature, yet all the while, Dakar continued to examine her as if she was looking for something.

"Do that again," the guest demanded.

"Do what?"

"Shrug your shoulders again; I think I saw something when your collar pulled open."

Doc stood up and glared down at the woman. "What are you talking about?"

"You have one too!" she exclaimed.

The woman clasped her hand to her neck and reared back. "Have one what!" Doc spouted. But her words fell before her sensible self could repair the error.

"A mark, the blue mark! If they see it, they'll arrest you." Dakar's voice was calculated and cold. The feeling of safety drifted away at that very moment as the icy threat fell upon the older woman like snow piling over a bank. Doc knew it could not snow forever, yet the sensation of smothering overwhelmed her, and while she envisioned gasping for air, she didn't hear the door open. Suddenly the sound of a dog panting filled her ears, and she was revived.

"You alright, Doc; you look really pale," Alabama remarked.

"She's okay," Dakar said. "We were just talking, and she forgot to tell me something. Didn't you?"

Doc attempted to present herself in an agreeable mood, but a sharp pang of reality stabbed at her temples. "I just have a bit of a headache." She lifted her eyes and saw that Trenton was not among them.

"Grandpa had to go," Alabama said. "He wanted to let you know he had to get back to work." The two women were cradling a secret, which Alabama felt he was interrupting. The voice in his head reminded him to be careful. It was one of those quiet times when nothing is spoken, but so much is said. Only Inja lapping water from the dog bowl created an ordinary moment accidentally inserted into this artificial gathering of friends.

"Dakar is leaving now." Doc resumed her position of authority and stood up. "Maybe you can help her with her backpack."

"Oh, don't bother, I can get it myself. I'm used to it," she said with an overly sweet smile. "I never take more than I can carry."

* * *

Mrs. Rivers had given the Senior Deputy quite enough time to decide. She was a good person and assumed she would be rewarded like the hopes of all good people. She didn't expect much, only what justice would offer a person of her humble means. But, after climbing several flights of stairs, the administrator's office was closed, and a handwritten sign reading, LUNCH BREAK, scribbled on yellow paper tacked to the door offered her time to gather her composure while those inside enjoyed their solitude. For she was an impatient woman and desired only one thing, to say her piece and get what she deserved. When you lose faith in something because you are human, you can lose faith in everything. So why had she trusted the occupiers? It was not a casual decision; her conclusion was the same as most of the population. Totalitarianism was preferable to chaos.

Mrs. Rivers was sure the men inside would open the door soon. After all, how long does it take to eat a cheese sandwich and coffee? She mentally prepared her role and decided to use her feminine vulnerability. The two brutes must have some passionate sympathy for a woman with two children. She would play to Senor Deputy's ego, imploring his good nature as a high-ranking official to accept her request, especially on her most recent merit.

But the woman was one of many petitioners, and upon hearing the bolt unlock, the address she had practiced suddenly flew out of her mind like a high school drama student. She knocked timidly, hearing an almost immediate, "Come in." Waiting an appropriate several seconds, she pulled open the door and walked into a sallow-colored office. Deputy Gris was behind his desk, still wearing a napkin. She smiled and pointed to his bib. He grumbled a few inaudible words and pulled the cloth aside. "You are?" he asked.

"Don't you remember?" asked the hurt woman, as if they had once been intimate.

"No, do you know this woman?" Gris asked his superior. Deputy Khanna turned his eyes up without raising his head and grunted. "Come forward, Madame, and tell me, what business you have with us?" demanded Gris.

Mrs. Rivers, now leaving behind her meek side, boldly turned away and walked to the oversized desk where Khanna was sitting like the master of the house filing his nails. "Don't you remember me?" she repeated, raising the ire of her impatience.

The Deputy set his nail file back in his desk and, taking pleasure in his rudeness, asked. "Should I?"

Shivers of resentment ran down her spine. "I'm Mrs. Rivers," she said, pulling her scarf off her head. Still, neither man gave her the satisfaction of recall. "Rivers," she said again. "I rid you of the witch," she announced.

"Ahhh, Rivers, yes, last week, the fire in the shed," Gris nodded as he spoke.

Senior Deputy Khanna shuffled a few papers and then looked up. "Yes, the report is here," he added, sliding his greasy finger across the document. "Your service had been noted." Then offering a perfunctory smile leaned back. "Is there anything else?"

The two-sidedness of the situation was taking its toll. "But you promised me," she said. "If I helped you, then you were to help me; that's what you said."

"Said, Mrs. Rivers, when did I say that!" demanded the Senior Deputy. "Gris, did you say that because I don't remember hearing any such thing." He turned back to the woman standing like a frail branch on a tree that was about to be cut free. "Tell me again, what we were to have promised you for fulfilling your part as a citizen?"

"My husband, all I want is for you to get him back home. I thought..." but at soon as she uttered these words, he cut them loose from her tongue.

"You thought, you thought, Madame, you do not need to think; we will do that for you!"

"But my husband!" she wailed.

"Your husband will return home when it is his time! As for your reward, your merit is recorded." A rush of excitement filled Khanna as his superiority roused him. "You do realize that I can report you," he added.

"Report me? What have I done?" Mrs. Rivers asked, her worrying hands turning pink.

"Bribery," he said.

"Bribery?" the meek woman asked. "How so?"

"It is quite obvious that you have something in your pocket you were going to offer," Khanna countered. "Here, empty your pockets, and I will show you!" Perplexed and now more than frightened, the woman began to whimper. Suddenly her entire body convulsed into heaves and sobs. "Stop your crying!" demanded the Deputy. Taken aback, Mrs. Rivers wiped her eyes on her sleeves and, like a wilting flower, drooped and, with intermittent sniffles, wavered. "If that is all, Mrs. Rivers," the indignant man howled, "I believe my next appointment will be arriving."

"Then there is no reward?" she whispered.

"Your reward, Madame, is that you are free to leave." There was a savageness about his reply, and when she closed the door behind her, she felt her positive emotions collapse and float away. Her goal crushed, her value structure usurped, all that remained attached was the feelings of distrust.

Chapter 18

Danube, the more cunning of the two sisters, decided all traces of Alice needed to be disposed of. And being of great imagination, tempted the younger with a walk to Doc's to trade in the drab gown for something else. What to choose would be determined by their findings. It wasn't until they started to bundle up the gown when a most curious label was found sewed into the collar.

"Polyester?" Amazon handed the dress back to her sister. "What does that mean?"

Danube fingered the label and read it again. "Polyester, maybe it's a place?"

They both sat for a moment perplexed. "Maybe it's a name. Maybe this dress belonged to someone named Polyester." Such an ingenious proposition gave Amazon reason to smile. But her suggestion didn't agree with the elder sister.

"No, I don't think so. I think it's where this was made. This label could be a clue as to where Alice was from."

"You mean after the moon!" Amazon chuckled.

But instead of looking sour, Danube became much more agreeable. "Yes, I bet she once lived in Polyester. In fact, the gown might bring us a better bargaining tool. It might be valuable, even if it is horribly ugly."

"Ugly!" protested Amazon, "I don't think it's ugly."

"Then what is it. It's the color of oatmeal and has absolutely no style? No, I really have to say it's ugly. It's a good thing it's from Polyester, or Doc wouldn't want it at all!"

Amazon, feeling dejected, had a difficult time convincing herself the garment wasn't ugly. It held a special meaning for her, having been Alice's, so she decided just to call it plain. She wrapped it in paper and taped it closed.

An uneasy feeling swept over the sisters as they walked past the crumbling remains of the garden. Within its borders were a few skinny bean stalks trying to hang on to life, and when they stopped to gawk, each girl sighed with exaggerated sympathy. The air around smelled sooty, not at all like nature was reclaiming its place. Instead, it seemed the earth had abandoned the garden, leaving behind a smell from the fiery act as a reminder. Neither girl wanted to think about their mother, but it was almost impossible to ignore her as being an arsonist. Yet, in the minds of the occupiers and neighbors, Mrs. Rivers was a heroine, someone that had single-handedly taken on the witch and preempted any sorcery. But Alice, a witch, was an absolutely ridiculous notion to the girls, even if she was strange.

They walked in the direction of Doc's; each taking turns carrying the bundle. "Mother is right," Amazon said, "it may never rain." And though they chattered about the weather, the talk strayed to the subject of Alice. However, their conversations never led to any lucid answers, only a dejected feeling they were responsible for her. She wasn't dead, but she was dead, concluding her history will be distorted if people believe she was a witch. On the other hand, a confession that they kept her hidden in the shed would again put her back in harm's way. "If we don't tell anyone, then they'll think she was evil!" Amazon fretted.

Danube disagreed. "But, if we explain about Alice, then Mother will have committed a crime because there was no witch."

"But Alice isn't dead, and Mother only set fire to the shed," Amazon tried to reason.

A moment of lucidity suddenly rose from this statement. "And, no one really knows who the witch is. As far as everyone believes there is no Alice, just a witch. For this reason, Alice never lived. We have no problem because she never really existed," explained Danube.

In all its strength, the sun finally hid behind a cloud offering a bit of a reprieve. "Well, I never imagined that I would feel so bad about someone. Let me see if I understand. Alice is not dead but is dead, and she never existed but does exist. I am getting confused," lamented Amazon.

"Me too," said Danube. "But we do know the truth."

"Which is?"

"Our responsibility is to keep Alice a secret."

"She did pretty well on her own without us," the younger sister remarked. But Danube pretended not to hear.

* * *

Amazon imagined Doc standing on her porch gazing over the sandy landscape. As they approach, the image of the woman drifts back inside, returning with a plate of cookies. Amazon conjured another bit of fiction from this story where the proprietor greets them with a pitcher of cold lemonade. But wishing is only that, a wish, and as they walked up to the door and knocked, the process of crafting such a delicious thought only thrust Amazon into disappointment despite her creative efforts. "What's the matter with you?" Danube asked, noticing her sister's serious expression.

However, before Amazon could answer, the door responded to their knock and opened. "So, you're back." Such a gruff delivery of sentiment to what was supposed to be a cheerful answer to the knock gave the sisters a feeling that perhaps they had made a mistake by coming.

The papered bundle hung limply in Danube's hand. "We came by to see if you had anything we could trade."

"I see," Doc said and smiled. "Well, if you don't mind dogs, come on in." Amazon caught her sister's look and followed her behind Doc. Inja, hearing the door to the stairwell open, joined the parade downstairs. "This is Inja," said Doc pointing to the dog. "She keeps an eye on things."

"Such a pretty dog!" exclaimed Danube, taking an immediate liking to the animal. "Where did you get her."

"From a boatman," explained Doc patting the dog on the head. "Okay, ladies, let's see what you've brought," Doc suggested eyeing their package. She escorted them to a table and pushed aside an empty crate occupying most of the space. Danube set the package down and split the paper open. "It's from polyester," she said, holding up the gown.

"Polyester?" Doc repeated. Danube handed her the dress as the woman flattened it against the paper wrapping.

"It's on the label," remarked Amazon. "See."

Doc picked the gown up again and, without speaking, nodded that she saw the printed label. "Where did you get this?" she asked.

"Get it?" Danube repeated.

"Yes, where did it come from."

"Polyester," smiled Amazon.

"Do you know where polyester is located?" Doc asked with dignified curiosity. But the question stumped both girls leaving them without an answer. "I was just wondering if your mother got you this gown or if you found it."

"Does it matter?" Danube asked. "All we want to do is trade it."

"And all I want to do is to find out where you got it."

"Does that mean it's valuable?" Amazon wanted to know.

"Well," said Doc. "That depends on what you mean as valuable. If you want to know its currency worth, I'd have to say, not any more than any other plain gown. But, if you mean valuable because of its origin, I will say yes."

The mood was uncomfortable. Neither of the sisters quite precisely understood what Doc was trying to say. "We got it from a friend," Danube admitted.

"Then why didn't your friend come to trade. Is she afraid?" Though small, Doc's question was boring a long hole into a place that was supposed to be secret.

"Because she left it with us, she didn't want it anymore." Danube felt good about her answer but picked up the garment and began to roll it up. "I guess we'll take this home since you don't seem to want to trade with us," she said gloomily. "I understand." Doc watched as the older sister carefully folded the paper around the gown. Danube kept her eyes on the dress, all the while feeling like an intrusion. "I think we should tell her," she blurted out. Then pulling the dress from the paper, she clutched the garment between her hands.

"We can't," Amazon squealed. "We promised."

"But we have to; someone needs to know."

"If you don't trust me, I think there is someone here that you might feel you can trust," Doc said. "But can I trust you to keep their secret?"

"Are they here now?" asked Amazon.

"That all depends on your answer. I'm a woman of my word. Are you women of your word?" She lowered her head and looked each girl in the eye. "Are you?" she whispered. Her hair fell forward, and as she brushed it back behind her shoulder, Amazon's face turned the color of paste; she was afraid. Yet, Danube was fearless and nodded in agreement. "What about you, Amazon? Can we trust you?" Doc peered at the girl waiting for an answer.

"Her name is Alice." Amazon's concession confirmed trust and obliterated it with one single word. Danube looked at her sister with astonishment. The answer was honest and dishonest, both at one instant, delivering a moral dilemma. Danube's thoughts fermented guilt as she searched for an excuse. She was equally as guilty as Amazon, even though she wasn't the one who blurted to Doc. Each sister had accepted an unsolicited invitation to trust Alice that embodied a promise to keep her a secret. As for Amazon, revealing the secret made her feel strangely different. Before, the truth she held gave her power, and now she was no longer in control; it had been relinquished to Doc.

"Alice, that's what she said her name was. She made up a lot of things, but she meant no harm." the older sister added, offering the bundled gown back to the woman. Trust didn't require obligation, so no harm was done.

"And so, you think Alice is from polyester. I can see why you might make that assumption. Only," Doc said, "polyester isn't a place. It's a kind of fabric, very rare. In fact, I don't think it's available anywhere around here."

"A fabric?" Danube repeated. Doc shook the crumpled gown open and spread it on the table. The elder sister read the label and then looked up timidly. "Polyester is not a place?" Doc nodded her head, no. "Well, I guess Alice's gown is from wherever she is from," said Danube. But in the second, after her simple explanation, this unwanted turn of events made her panic. There were too many questions, too many strange answers, and at once, she felt trapped by her knowledge. She would say no more for fear that they believed she was a witch. The dress lay on the table, a symbol of Alice's nonpresence.

The girls appeared afraid, Amazon holding Danube's arm, her eyes fixed on the gown. She felt as if her whole being sagged like a limp flower when something cold and wet nudged her leg. Inja sat by her side and wagged her tail. "She likes you," Doc said. Amazon allowed herself to laugh and bent down to pet the dog that promptly replied by grabbing the gown off the table scampering away into the stairwell.

"The dress!" shrieked Amazon starting after the dog, "she's got Alice's dress!" A bit of a commotion ensued as Danube followed her sister and the taunting dog, but none got very far because someone kept them from entering through the threshold.

∗ ∗ ∗

It was Alabama blocking the way. Inja dropped the dress at his feet. "It belongs to Alice," Amazon cried as the boy picked up the dress, a bit soggy where Inja had carried it in her mouth.

"What are you doing with it?" he asked.

"We were going to trade it until the dog snatched it off the table." By now, everyone but Inja about-faced and returned to the blue room.

"Say, what are you doing here?" asked Danube suspiciously. "I thought you were in hiding."

"I am," said Alabama. "But you didn't answer my question about the dress."

"Alice has gone off and left us with her stuff, so we decided we better get rid of it before...," but the elder sister's voice dropped away, leaving her thought incomplete.

"Before what?" demanded Alabama.

"Before they got into trouble and had to tell the authorities what they know," explained Doc, standing unnoticed by the curio shelf. "Fortunately, they came here." The woman looked at the girls and then back to Alabama. "They told me about Alice."

The source of their fear vanished with finding Alabama. What they had gathered and carried around was passed over. Silence would remain not unlike before; only the burden became weightless. "We had to tell," Amazon said, turning to Alabama. "But only to Doc."

"What are you going to pick out for your trade?" he asked, trying to turn the attention away from himself.

Amazon sighed with delight. "I don't know," she exclaimed. But Danube already had an idea; there was something in the room that she wanted. She had seen it before when they had come the first time, in the large oak cabinet behind a pair of glass doors.

"What about you, Danube?" Doc asked, dangling the question like bait.

The question stunned the elder sister, for it came at the precise moment her mind had wandered from the group. "Me?"

"Yes, what would like to trade for?" Danube did not hesitate and walked over to the cabinet. Eyelevel to the shelf, she peered through the dusty glass. "Open it," said Doc watching the girl. Danube looked over, and Doc insisted again, "Open the doors." Gingerly, Danube obliged and tugged on the small knob releasing the door from its closed position. Then without having to search, she saw the shell exactly where she remembered it had been waiting and removed it from the shelf.

"This," she said.

"What is it?" exclaimed her sister. "Let me see!" Then, hurrying over, Amazon meandered around the table to her sister.

"Careful!" whispered Danube; "it's fragile." Tenderly, she placed it into Amazon's hands.

"What is it?" Amazon asked.

Doc laughed, "I see you found my shell."

"It's a shell," Danube echoed.

Amazon made a scowl. "I heard, but what's it for?"

Danube shrugged and then snatched it back. "Look closely, it has perfectly coiled spirals. I like it." Amazon wasn't sure if trading for this shell was as good a deal as they might get. "She only has this one," Danube whispered. Amazon nodded, rethinking her initial idea. "Where'd you get it?" Danube asked, walking over to Doc. She opened her palm to display her find.

"My cerith," Doc explained. "It's from the wilderness, not the wilderness, you know. Shells like this one were found and harvested in the ocean."

"The ocean!" cried Amazon. "You've been near the ocean?" The younger sister grew fearful. "Oh, we were told of how dangerous the ocean is!"

"It's not so dangerous," said Doc. "When I was young my family always went to the ocean." A lament framed her statement. "But this is all I have left of my time there. This cerith shell is only valuable because of the memories it holds. There is an old story about a man; he lived a century or more ago. His name was Theodore Grant. He traveled in a covered wagon from the east coast's seaside to the prairie to bring the ocean to the people. His story is rooted with a love of the sea." Doc lifted the shell. "I must say, Danube, you have a good eye. Most pass this by." She handed the shell back.

"So, we can trade?" said Danube.

Doc's moment was tangled; she was an unsentimental person feeling uncharacteristically sentimental. Wind and storms may tear up the earth, but they can never tear free what lies within the person. But she had seen the ocean; the cerith had sacrificed enough. "Yes," said the woman, "I think it's a fair deal, the shell for the polyester gown. But you haven't answered one question. Alice, did she look different from your other friends?"

This question put to the sisters was not for sale. "Different?" repeated Danube. "She was kind of skinny."

"And messy, yes, sometimes messy," said Amazon.

However, Doc was not satisfied with their quips. "What about a mark? Did she have any unusual marks?"

"Like freckles? No, no freckles," Amazon added trying to smile. But the invisible bond hiding the secret was inching away. The confines of the spacious room, where one could travel freely, look, and remove any object offered liberation to speak freely.

"You can trust Doc," Alabama said. "She's on our side."

Out of the shadow, Inja appeared, approaching the table with its tail wagging. *If only I could be as trusting as this dog,* *Amazon thought.*

"What if we tell you? How do we know you won't tell the occupiers?" Danube asked.

"Because if she has what I think she has, she's in more danger than you care to imagine," replied Doc.

Now it was Alabama that appeared confused. Turning to Doc, his demeanor solicited a response. "What could they know about Alice that would be suspicious?"

"Truth is known, and authentic truth experienced." Doc pulled her hair aside and, lowering her collar, pulled it aside. "Did she have a mark like this?" she asked, exposing a small blue tattoo. Neither girl spoke up, yet their profound expression, pale and resigned, acknowledged what the woman believed to be true.

"I don't understand," said Alabama. "What's going on?"

"Nothing is going on," Doc said. "I just wanted to know if Alice had a mark on her neck too. But, now that I have found out, there's nothing more I want to know. Alice is obviously a brave girl, but sometimes even the most courageous need help."

"But that mark, you have one too," insisted Alabama.

"It's no big deal!" Danube interrupted.

"Yea, what's the big deal, lots of people have weird moles," exclaimed Amazon.

The shell was more than an object; it was a bond. Danube held the cerith tightly. Doc did not make them divulge the secret about Alice, yet she sacrificed herself to find out. But by doing so, she acknowledged her trust in the sisters. As if standing on a frozen pond, the ice beneath them cracked. The silent fissure created led them all to move carefully. It had been a long day; it was time to go home.

* * *

Alabama listened to Doc before the pair of sisters arrived and before he departed into the night with the dog. Doc was age, and he was youth, and as much as we would like to distinguish youth as becoming and age as is, we will consider both as a portrait in flux. Alabama transfixed all attention on Doc when she presented the question that had no spontaneous response, for it left no shadow of a hint to aim for. "How might a person live?" A curious question, open-ended leading to so many possibilities. Unlike a lecture, 'Live this way,' the silence in the kitchen advanced without assurance of an answer. Should and might were different and the same, depending upon the response.

On the kitchen wall opposite to the stove, the pots hung with their shiny copper bottoms out. Three, to be exact. They were arranged with the care one takes with a picture in a frame, strategically positioned over the counter in arms reach without having to strain. Alabama sat rigidly in his seat. "I know you're anxious to leave, and I think you should, but not in the same manner you arrived," she said. "The world is changing, as we all are. And as much as you have recognized yourself as a product of an identity prescribed by your surroundings, identity is not rigid. You must allow it to emerge from becoming; you will always be in the process of being." Alabama scarcely understood. Doc had a way of talking that never seemed to say anything which made sense, and as much as he tried to follow her logic, the reasoning didn't show up. So, he remained fixed on her face and decided not to move his mouth, preventing him from showing any signs of confusion. That is until she said, "Do you follow?"

"Not really."

But his answer did not deter her from continuing down this thorny path. "I asked you a hypothetical question, 'How might a person live?' I can't tell you how for no one knows the answer. But I don't want you to cling to the present as a baby kangaroo. Instead, allow yourself to advance and embrace what is different. You are just a single perspective in the universe. Take the call to action. You'll never know what it is to be, just what it is to become."

His eyes met hers, and he thought he saw her almost smile. "That's good," he said. "Because I don't know what to do if I stay, but I do know if I leave."

"Just remember, the world owes you nothing, so don't wait for it. You have values, but the values you have should not lead you to become complacent or conform to the ideals of others. The authoritarians wield power by luring those beneath them to adopt their values. Subservience is the destiny of the followers."

* * *

He left that night with the dog. He would follow Alice's rhyme even if the words were ambiguous, but then, aren't all words?

We can never have perfect clarity of meaning because words are always hidden behind the never-ending chain of definitions. They're constantly on the move, being analyzed, interpreted, and assigned to another subtext. Yet, Alabama decided he would try to follow Alice's rhyme of words. Their literal context originated from her voice; however, once released, they assumed a whole new earthy realm to unwrap by way of past and future translations. To understand the true meaning is seemingly impossible since the words are both parasitic and dominating depending upon the user. From one idea, another is opened, rather like an infinite pandora's box. Alabama knew he had a daunting task which he naively was ready to take on.

* * *

The world is not furnished with ready-made meaning; we are responsible for creating that meaning.

Chapter 19

Dakar Hamlet's assignment to disrupt the banking system was far from complex. By flooding the market with an influx of stolen seed currency and clearing a path for change, the occupied citizens could finally reject the national currency. An attempt to reestablish the national banking system would irrevocably be challenged by smaller territorial banks established by black market hoarding. This rudimentary plan, which the renegades had already set into motion with the recent robbery at the seed bank, was slowly releasing pollinated varieties into the population.

The woman paused a moment, then, assuming her identity as a loyalist, she pushed her bicycle into the rack and locked the wheel to the post. In the endeavor to show goodwill, Dakar purchased some cake for the Senior Deputy and his assistant, knowing that a full stomach is always a way to win over one's trust. The bakery box had teetered on the handlebars, and though the road was stony, she managed to arrive at the station without a single piece of cake breaking.

Senior Deputy Khanna was sitting behind the desk when Dakar opened the door. His eyes sparkled with delight when she set the box before him. "What's the occasion?" he asked. The prospect of sweets changed his general grimace into sudden admiration for the day. "My life has taught me not to expect much, but a box like this placed before me is either for a birthday, which it is not, or good news." Gris, who had been pouring over papers when the woman entered, looked over with envious eyes. He yawned, attempting not to appear interested.

"I have a bit of interesting news," Dakar answered and, with the letter opener, split the twine. She opened the box, tilting it forward to display the lemon cream-filled cake. Like sunshine that emerges after a long rain, the appearance of dessert lightened what would ordinarily be a dull and boring afternoon.

"So, what news have you got, Dakar?" Khanna asked between bites. His cheeks, puffed like a chipmunk in winter, were working overtime. "Delicious," he said, licking his fingers, and greedily took the second piece of cake intended for Gris. "Seniority," he laughed and stuffed his mouth.

The forlorn Deputy smiled meekly, silently lamenting his loss but pretending not to care; he spoke up. "The news, what's your news?"

"I have a source," she said lying, "that has reliable information concerning the newcomer walking through the frontier. And the boy you're looking for, he's headed in the same direction."

Upon hearing this, Khanna sat up, brushing the crumbs from his lap. Then he gestured for Dakar to have a seat. It was obvious he was interested. "And where did you come up with this information?" A more uninviting creature could not have been seated across from her. He continued to suck the sugar from his fingers as he waited for her to answer.

"That, I won't tell," she said. "But if you want to take my advice and keep Colonel Yukon content, you'll follow up with my claim. I'm confident between you and Deputy Gris; an apprehension will lead to an arrest and perhaps a promotion."

"What do you mean you won't tell," Khanna repeated. This time he stood up and leaned forward. "I hope you have not forgotten that the authorities will be asking me where I got this information before they allow me to continue."

Dakar didn't budge. If she intended to get the two men to trust her, she would have to call his bluff. If she gave up a name so quickly, they would surely know she could not be trusted with internal information. "I won't tell," she said and pushed her chair back.

"Not so fast," exclaimed Gris. "Where in the frontier?"

"The western path into the dry river. A family of peddlers was stopped on the border before entering the trade region. Bear in mind; their information was reluctantly provided."

"And the boy? How do you know he's also heading in that direction?" Khanna asked with an icy stare.

"Instinct," she said.

"Instinct? Then what you believe is not certain," Gris muttered with disgust.

"On the contrary. My belief is necessarily true, so it can't be false," Dakar countered. "Reality is independent of what you or I think; it's outside the mind, so any decisions either of you makes are not yours."

"As are yours, Hamlet," replied Khanna. "However, I do applaud you for coming forward. I suppose it wouldn't hurt to look into the matter." Not forgetting his yearning for a better placement, he was anxious to gratify his superior, Colonel Yukon, a brute of a man. "These peddlers, how reliable are they?"

"As reliable as anyone. It is worth mentioning that the family has no reason to lie."

The answer did not offer Khanna much confidence; the citizens were all liars. Khanna drummed the desk with his knuckles, a habit he did when trying to make a decision. False claims were often grossly misrepresented, as was bad information. Moreover, his position was at stake, meaning he might get the promotion he deserved if they apprehended the boy or the newcomer. The idea Dakar planted brimmed with an eager response. "Gris!' he shouted, "get me the chief inspector; we have a job to do!"

Part V

Alice's Journey

Chapter 20

"It would help me," Alice thought, "if I knew which beginning to assign myself. Is it before or after Blank? Both coincide with this place I'm leaving and being faced with an impossible situation; I can only guess I got caught in an hourglass. I started at one end and then squeezed through to the opposite side. There is no way to explain my existence historically because if I close my eyes, I'm in the past, and when I open my eyes, I'm in the past." She stood on the edge of the open road dressed in clothes she had taken from Danube; beige-colored pants and a pale blue shirt, and though it was missing a button on the collar, it fit her well enough. Her feet were larger than either girl, so the mother's canvas shoes stuffed with some paper in the toe suited her just fine.

The question of her departure revealed to herself that maybe she was not leaving for good and may come back one day. The sky had taken on the color of oatmeal, and she wondered if it was dying. A shroud of clouds gradually merged, settling above with no intention of allowing the sun to pass through. Such a sky was more than gloomy. "It must be my mood," Alice thought. "In the confines of the shed, the sky was always blue; one can always have a blue sky if they don't see it." Her thoughts turned into punctuated monologues of commas but no full stops. Punctuation riddled with periods required being tethered to one place. She thought of her father's ring of keys in his pocket; wherever he went, he carried the keys. "It takes a great deal of discipline to be in charge of keys," Alice said. "But unless you have a door to open, keys are an unnecessary burden for the doorless."

The road ahead was dusty and narrow. Traces of wheeled vehicles occupying its boundaries of scrubby shallow weeds had forged grooves down the center. Her eyes followed as far as the horizon where the sandy-colored road met the pale sky. As a mirage rose above the imaginary line, Alice watched the wiggly illusion. She recalled their garden in the early mornings as if washed in dew the night before. Alice turned away from the parched road and walked in the direction of the fairy rings. "I do hope the mole is in the right temperament to take me on." And like an uprooted pansy in winter, she was gone.

* * *

Not a flower wavered in the breeze because there were no flowers or breeze. The stirring of silence touched Alice, and as she walked, it offered her youthful curiosity reason to pause. Upon a large rock sat a cadaver; however, as she inched toward it, she realized it was not what she thought but merely a bent figure possessed in a most supine manner. This stranger, a woman or a man was dressed in rags, and a headdress made of the same flimsy cloth twirled around the head, lowered just above the eyebrows. The individual turned their head up slightly, catching Alice staring. As if preparing all physical strength, it grimaced at the sight of the youth. "Go away."

"Well, I certainly can't leave you like this," said Alice. "Although, I am not sure what state of affairs you are really in."

The ragged individual summoned its voice, first with a cough and then by remarking, "Let me be."

"That is a declaration we can all agree upon," Alice said. "I know for myself, I wish to be, yet the more I search, the more I realize I just may never find me."

"My state of affairs," the ragged one claimed, "is despondency. My health is not, and now that you've heard my woes, be off with you," and lifting a bony hand, pointed a finger in the direction away from the rock it was sitting on.

"Have you seen a doctor?" asked Alice trying her best to offer compassion.

"Doctors, they're all quacks!" complained the poor wretch. "I have taken countless and useless elixirs and potions. I have been poked and prodded. My pains are great and my hunger greater." Alice nodded her head in understanding. Such words, she could not dispute, having remembered the old man. The grandfather could be cured, but despondency? Even her white pills would not work.

"I think I have something to help," Alice said. Reaching into her pocket, she removed a pouch and opened it up with just enough of a slit to pinch something from within its mouth.

"What have you got there?" snapped the ill person continuing in an irritated tone.

But ignoring the statement, Alice took her time pawing through the pouch. Finally, she returned the small bag into her pocket and opened her clenched hand. "I believe this will help you." She walked towards the rock and held up her outstretched palm. The invalid's eyes retrieved what she held. "I don't want to give you false hopes," Alice said. "Still, if you want to try, it might help."

"What is it?" asked the wretch, snatching the object up and rolling it over their dirty palm. Then they peered down. "Why should I believe you?" The speaker complained with such an abrupt outburst that Alice wasn't sure if she should reply.

"I suppose you have no reason to," Alice said. "But if I believe your testimony, that all remedies failed miserably, then the testimony I am offering you is equally valid."

"Will this work?" asked the doubter. "It's nothing more than a grey stone and very ordinary looking at that."

"If you have doubts, then I cannot help. But, if you have confidence in my treatment, there is positive hope for curing you of despondency."

"How long will it take?" the ragged person asked.

Alice shrugged. "I don't know." She could not affirm. The object she offered is a stone, which most likely broke off from a rock that broke from a boulder, like the one the tattered person was sitting on. If so, this stone was once part of the landscape, part of a more expansive terrain, part of the region, the moon, the solar system, the cosmos, infinity. Alice decided it best not to dwell on the matter, and now that the ragged person had taken ownership of the stone, the cure was really nothing more than confidence.

The poor wretch rolled the stone around in his mouth, sucking on it as if it were hard candy. Then spitting out the rubble, placed it snuggly between the folds of the headband. "You are my benefactor, the only person who has shown me any kindness since the counterfeit government took over." No sooner did Alice hear these words did she turn away from the ragged individual. "Where are you going?" called the rock sitter.

"I'm following the mole," she said.

"I suggest you find the shortest route," the melancholy person said.

"Why would I?" asked Alice. "If I do, then I will gain time, as well as lose time in the process, in addition to avoiding something that I don't know exists. Therefore, I'm afraid that I'm unable to take your recommendation." By now, the rumpled person demonstrated little energy towards the conversation and lay in the sun like a lizard. It has been a most rewarding experience, Alice decided, and hoped there would be others as accommodating.

* * *

Beneath a sky grey and twilight,
Where shrubs and creepers intertwine,
Our cozy stands, well roofed with leaves,
And there we sleep till morn

* * *

The wild grass resembled wheat stalks from a distance, but as she crossed a shaded path, the stalks of golden chaff were not what they seemed. The field's colors moved in the pewter light, playing tricks with the sunlight. Alice stood next to the millet grass and measured its height as more than shoulder high. She pulled on one of the bottlebrush stems, catching a handful of seeds as her palm ran down the stalk. While depositing the remains in a cloth pouch, she did not see the crooked shadow walking towards her on the path.

A sort of guttural groan made her look up. Neither tall nor short, because of the bent carriage, the figure ambled with a limping gait. He wore an unrecognizable uniform, one that had seen years of wear. The pants and shirt, once dark blue, had faded and was adorned with two striped lapels, red, white, and navy. The left shoulder's lapel was torn from the shirt and dangled with just enough thread to keep it from breaking free. "What brings you to this outer region?" asked the man, and as he wandered closer, Alice could see his cap frayed at the brim, shielded a scruffy face with eyes blinking from the sunlight.

"I'm looking for the fairy rings," Alice said. "Now that I have found the location of these wild grasses, they shouldn't be far."

He began to follow her search without moving, for it pained him to walk. "Have you been looking long?" he asked, now finding it tiresome to watch her weave between the plants.

"Long? I don't know," Alice said, retrieving a snail from the earth. "Long enough for me to find him." Then placing the tiny creature on the soil, she stepped back onto the dirt path.

"I understand," the man said. "I have been waiting, but not for fairy rings," he laughed.

"I should think not," exclaimed Alice. "You appear to know where you are going. I, on the other hand, am going, not where you are going."

"I am not going," exclaimed the man, and while removing his rag of a cap, displayed a fluff of white hair. "I was not always white-haired," he confessed.

"I wouldn't think so," replied Alice honestly. "It would have been very unusual if you always did." Alice examined the whole man with more scrutiny than he was using on her. "Are you a soldier, or have you just borrowed the uniform from one?" she asked.

Taken aback by her question, the bent-over man appeared to grow in height. "I am a soldier and a damn good one at that." Then, with a mighty walrus-like grunt, he resumed his narrative as if on cue. "For two cold winter months, we, me and the 86th battalion, held the center flank against the occupiers. But to our bad luck, the snow was relentless that November, and our food supply nearly depleted. That's when more than half of our own trusted soldiers, serving under our flag, revolted against us, deserting their posts and surrendering to the occupiers. All for a bowl of stew!" Again, the walrus bark sounded as he cleared his throat, giving him a moment to rearrange his tale. "Our own soldiers declared enemies, disgracing the country by turning yellow. Who can you confide in, I ask?"

The old soldier's lamentation distracted Alice from her hunt for fairy rings. However, it would be callous to ignore the pause in the story without her asking, "Then what happened?"

"We were captured and deported to a labor camp. For ten years, I remained in exile while promises of leniency were made to the occupied citizens. But these were only lies designed to keep the people in check. Bah! All sentimental rubbish. Nothing will change until the whole country becomes a smoldering hotbed of sedition." His eyes pierced like a wild cat.

"So, how did you come to this place?" Alice asked.

"I found it by chance. One night, I set out walking with no location in mind but to travel as far into the frontier as I could. I think I've been walking most of my life since being released from the labor camp. And so, here I am."

Alice studied the old soldier with kindness but without pity. "I'm not sure, but I don't think you are here." She smiled and began to look between the tall grasses for the fairy rings.

"What do you mean, not here. I'm here aren't I!" the confused fellow exclaimed, pointing to the dusty spot where he stood.

Alice turned and walked back to the middle of the path. "Only for a moment because once you move, here is there. Watch," she said. "I am here, but as I move," which she did with exaggeration, stretching her gangly legs with long strides. "That here is now there. So, you can never be here, for very long. I'm afraid you will be traveling a long time, maybe forever, to get to the here you want now."

The soldier appeared baffled as he ruminated over what he had just heard. "Well," he finally said with a trifle of discouragement, "I better be on my way if I ever want to get from there to here."

"I agree," remarked Alice. "It was very nice to make your acquaintance."

"Likewise, my dear, likewise. I hope you find what you're looking for; it can be rather daunting."

＊ ＊ ＊

They pawned away all their land
A hut they left behind
A goodly place to take a rest
And sleep until sunrise

＊ ＊ ＊

The first pulse of dawn summoned the blackbirds as they tottered about looking for food. The soil, moist and black, camouflaged the earthworms as they dodged their predators' beady eyes. "You know where Mr. Mole is too," Alice said, lifting the wriggly creature onto her palm. "You've traveled through his tunnels." She placed the worm back on the soil, and in a moment, it had collapsed the earth around itself. "You had better be careful; Mr. Mole may eat you for breakfast!" she warned, but the worm was too far beneath the soil to answer.

Having located Mr. Mole, Alice removed the compass from her pocket and rotated the dial until the arrow pointed north. Then, steadying the instrument started in the direction of the mound. But she did not get very far when a small caravan of merchants following one behind the other was heading from the south. Now, if she were in a city, it would not have been so unusual, but on a lowly path, barely wide enough for a pedestrian, the group appeared out of place. "What have you got there, missy?" called the merchant from behind his rickety pushcart.

Alice lowered the compass and quickly put it back in her pocket, retrieving a lumpy rock in its place. "My lucky rock," she said, holding it up for the fellow to see.

"Lucky?" inquired a woman, trying to get a better view. "Bring it here; I've never seen a lucky stone." The entourage of five stopped as if in unison, all very interested in what Alice was holding.

"What's she got?" shouted a yellow-bearded fellow at the end of the procession.

"Some sort of rock," said his wife, seemingly annoyed by the entire incident, for she was pushing a handcart with wheels unsuited for the path.

"Perhaps you would like to make a trade," welcomed the head merchant. And with enthusiastic gusto, gestured to Alice. "We are the Paris family," he said. "There is my wife," pointing to a slender petite woman wearing a green dress with smocking, over there my sister and her husband and their baby, London, on his back. And who are you?" Mister Paris asked with great curiosity. "We rarely see anyone in the frontier except for the settlers."

"Alice," said the youth.

"Alice," piped in the wife. "What kind of a name is that?"

"Excuse my wife, she can be nosey," replied Mister Paris, discouraging his wife from any more outbursts. "What she meant to say was Alice is a very unusual name."

"I meant nothing of the kind," snapped the rude woman. "We can't be too careful, and a name like that could mean trouble."

"Trouble?" replied Alice, toying with the woman. "Oh, I never have trouble since I always carry with me my lucky stone." She held it up to the sunlight rotating it as if holding a gold nugget. "No, no trouble at all."

At once, the sister and husband came over to see what was going on. He walked with care as the chubby baby slept strapped to his back. "May I hold your lucky stone?" inquired the yellow-bearded man. The baby stirred restlessly as he walked. "Maybe some of the good luck will rub off on me," he implored.

Alice started to place it in his palm and then quickly snatched it back. "I'm not sure if I should," she said.

"Why not?" asked the brother-in-law with disappointment.

"It's just seeing that you are a merchant; perhaps you might give me something in exchange for a bit of luck."

"She does have a point," Mr. Paris agreed. "After all, it only seems only fair." All the others nodded in agreement.

"Well, what do you want?" asked the fellow.

"The way to the old Mill Creek," Alice said.

"The old what?" asked the sister.

"Mill Creek," Alice repeated.

A curious murmur followed as each family member tried to decipher the information. Finally, Mr. Paris took off his cap, stroked his black hair, and then plopped the cap back on as if having come up with an answer. "Mill?" he said. "I'm afraid that doesn't register. We've been traveling this region all our lives and mill; can't say we know what that means. What about you, sister. You went to school. What's a mill?"

"A mill," she cleared her throat and paused. "A mill is," but nothing came to mind. Again, a consensus of misinformation assembled in all their heads as they waited for the sister. "Mill," the woman repeated aloud, but with greater emphasis than before, "mill is an abbreviation for millage. And millage is a rate of tax! And a mill is a small portion of a tax." Suddenly a collective gasp rang out.

"Tax!" cried the wife, "I knew it; you're a tax collector!" Then, again, the word tax generated a unanimous groan.

"And to think we trusted you," lamented Mr. Paris.

But the statement surrendered little emotion from Alice, who continued to barter. "Well, can you lead me in the direction of the creek," she asked.

"Then you don't want a tax?" Mrs. Paris asked with relief.

"Certainly not," said Alice. "What would I do with a tax? I barely have enough room in my sack for my possessions. Besides, a tax for what? You can't go around demanding a tax if you haven't anything of value."

"Now see here," grumbled the bearded man, "Let's not get insulting. Our goods are worthy of a tax; in fact, they are even worthy of a tariff. Just look here," he said, holding up a faded cap. "It may not look like much, but it's authentic."

"Authentic what?" asked Alice inspecting the material.

"An authentic cap. Why look at the brim; without it, it would not be a cap. It would simply be a beanie."

Alice could not argue with that. It was truly an authentic cap, and so she put it on. "Well, since you cannot tell me where the mill is, I will take the cap in exchange for your incorrect answer. And the creek?" she asked. "You may hold the lucky stone if you can tell me about the creek."

Mr. Paris thought for a moment and passed a glance to the others. He gave a doubtful look at Alice and sighed. "There's a well not too far from where we're headed," he said. "You're welcome to join us if you like."

"I'm afraid a well will not fulfill my needs," Alice retorted. "You see, it is a creek that I need to find."

"My poor husband, I am afraid he'll never get to hold the lucky rock," the woman added with a tone of indifference. Luck was merely something other people were endowed with.

The frontier for Alice was a land humming with silent opportunities and dark tunnels underground. She looked past the family and at the mounds. Her imagination raced ahead at the dusty landscape. *His favorite game is hide and seek; find him at the old mill creek, Travel at an easy pace, Until the stones are out of place.* "Well, if you don't know," Alice said, "I'll be on my way." She shrugged her shoulders and started to place the stone into the sack.

Mr. Paris grunted as he began to lift the cart's handles up off the ground. "Creek, creek, creek," he muttered as he waited for the rest of the entourage to gather their wares. Then with several perfunctory utterances, he suddenly exclaimed, "I've got it! Creek, yes, remember?" he cried to his wife, almost causing her to tumble over with his exuberance. "The meadowland, it changed, or so my grandmother told me. There was a creek, but that was before our day. Alice!" he bellowed. But by now, Alice was on a leisurely pace several meters past the yellow-bearded man and the chubby baby, who was wide-eyed and playing with a string on its bonnet. "Miss! Stop walking!"

More than out of breath, Mr. Paris ran up the path. "I must tell you," he shouted, "there is no creek!" Alice waited while Mr. Paris took several large breaths. "The creek," he said, "yes, there was once a creek long before my day. But after the occupiers took over, they rerouted the water, built many bastions, and a garrison along what was the bank." Alice appeared remarkably unshaken by his revelation. "Do you understand, there is no creek," he confirmed. "Just a dry runlet, no mud, no sludge; waterless."

"There is no creek?" Alice remarked. "When you tell me the creek is not, it's because that's what you perceive the creek to be; that's your truth. But for me, a creek is not restricted by your interpretation. So how can you define the creek by what you said it is not?" Mr. Paris said nothing, but his cheeks took on a rosy hue. "By any chance, did the creek move?" Alice asked.

"Certainly not; it is exactly where we left it; about a day's walk from this very spot we are standing on?" Mr. Paris said. "Only it is as dry as a bone and covered with thorny scrubs."

To dilute the man's noble efforts were harsh, but Alice had not set out to try and change his mind. "I'm afraid I disagree with you, Mr. Paris. Even though I have no image of the creek, neither past, present, or future, I can only draw on the information I have traced. If the location remains fixed, then this creek, which we are both speaking of, is. My meaning and your meaning are both true since neither of us is deceiving the other. We'll never establish a perfect meaning since we can't escape chasing our intentions."

"And what would that be?" Mr. Paris questioned, trying not to appear perplexed.

"Determining perfect clarity. The creek is bigger than consciousness." Alice smiled. "We can, however, part knowing we are both correct."

By now, the brother-in-law had walked to where Alice and Mr. Paris were standing without disturbing the baby. Except for a few "waw waws," the contained child remained very peaceful, almost inanimate. The yellow-bearded fellow sighed deeply when Alice looked over. She reached into her pouch and rummaged about appearing to locate the item. "I have to be on my way," she acknowledged retrieving the lucky stone.

"I must say, you are a very complicated person. I think most of what you said makes sense," Mr. Paris chuckled under his breath. "We also must be getting on with our journey." The two women remaining with the carts leerily observed the goings-on up the path. Each hoping the lucky stone would come into their possession.

"Here," said Alice to the bearded man. "You've been very patient. You may keep my lucky stone." And with an outstretched hand, she held the grey rock out for him; but instead of taking it, he backed away. A curious expression came over the youth as she suddenly realized he didn't want it.

"No, thank you," the brother-in-law said. "I think you may need it more than any of us. You're just one, and our luck is multiplied five times."

"He's right," said Mr. Paris. "Put it back in your pouch; you may need it if you plan to travel farther into the frontier."

Chapter 21

Ⅰt was very hot. It seemed always to be hot. Alabama and Inja planned to travel most of the afternoon until a storm of gossamer dust and sand hindered their intentions, and they sought shelter beside an oblong boulder. They rested for a while, and when the dust subsided, they continued. They hadn't walked for very long when Alabama made out the silhouette of a hut in the flat expanse. A most welcome sight for these two vagabond travelers. Dusk brought a sour odor, and the boy thought it might be loneliness he smelled. He had never felt lonely until now. But the dog soon lapped up that bleakness when she scampered ahead with her wagging tail raised high.

By the time they reached the hut, the sky had claimed all the colors, for the small dwelling appeared strangely pink in the dusky hue. The door hung limply on its rusted hinges, and although it gave the impression as being unsound, it was solid. Confessing to himself his weariness, Alabama did not hesitate to pull the latch when, not to his surprise, the door opened, and he peered into the darkening room. However, unlike what he expected, it was not vacant. In the corner was the shadow of a man sitting in a cane chair. Alabama could not make out the face, nor could he tell if the person was old or young, but what he could see was the chin rested on his chest, and every few moments, the entire body would move up and down as he exhaled and inhaled. He was asleep.

Inja pulled free from Alabama's light hold on her collar and walked over to the seated figure. She sniffed his feet and then made a lap around the room before returning to the boy. Alabama watched the limp figure for a few minutes and decided that if he hadn't woken by now, there was no harm in sharing the space for the night. The hut offered little refuge from the heat. Alabama sat at the edge of the cot, which stood on rickety legs. He wondered why the man chose to sleep in the chair, supposing it was because the fellow had thought he was only staying long enough to rest his legs. A heave of evening light settled, making room for darkness. He could hear panting; he could hear the man snoring; he could hear a voice in his head. *Along the lonely countryside, Golden wheat grows shoulder high, Where Mr. Mole makes fairy rings, And up above the blackbirds sing.* Alabama listened for the birds, but there were none. Then, he did a most out of the ordinary thing; he whistled. Inja came scampering over and pushed her nose against the boy's arm. That was when the smell of loneliness disappeared.

* * *

Inja was the first to awaken, not because of the morning light but because she was a dog, and dogs do those kinds of things. And it was not the nudging of her nose against the boy but her loud yawn that woke the boy from his sleep. He sat up and remembered where he was. The chair that had been occupied during the evening was vacant, except for a hat and canvas shoulder bag on the seat. Alabama put on his shoes and let Inja out. He stood in the open doorway and watched his four-legged companion disappear around the corner. But instead of Inja, the man reappeared. "There's an outhouse around back," the white-haired fellow exclaimed, "and a pump. The water's pretty cold, but I'm used to that. Got enough coffee if you want any." His bent gait was slow, and as he walked, he barely lifted his eyes, but his voice was strong. The boy stepped aside and then followed him into the hut.

"This your place?" Alabama asked.

"Was going to ask you the same thing," the older man said.

"You a soldier?" Alabama asked.

"I guess you could say so but haven't seen real action in quite a while. Ever heard of the 86th Battalion? That was my men and me."

"My grandfather was in the resistance too, but I don't think he could fit into his uniform anymore."

The old veteran laughed. "I knew you were trustworthy; any man that would share space with a stranger and not wake him up can't be bad. I don't see many people on my travels. Nice to talk to someone."

"Where you headed?" Alabama asked.

"That's the problem. I'm here, and when I leave to go there, I end up here."

Alabama appeared confused. "Maybe you're walking in a circle," he suggested.

Now it was the soldier who appeared perplexed. "No, I don't think so. Last night was the first time in this hut. Let me explain. If I walk there," he said, pointing across the floor, "when I get to that spot, I am here. It happens every time. At this rate, I'll never get there."

The boy scratched his chin and nodded. "I see what you mean. You sound like the friend I'm looking for. It's likely she came by this hut too, seeing that it's on the way."

"On the way?" questioned the old man. "On the way to what?"

"The way of this path." The cadence in his voice gave way to his own translation of the way, although the old soldier didn't seem to concern himself with the reply and continued without toying with its nuances.

"This friend, was she a girl about so high?" the old man asked, raising his flat palm to the tip of his chin. "The young lady I met said she was looking for fairy rings. I thought it was kind of odd until I realized what she meant, moles."

"Yes!" cried Alabama, "that's Alice! How long ago did you speak with her?"

The old soldier studied the ceiling as if searching for the answer. "Must have been a few days ago. But she wasn't in any kind of a hurry, so if you're on her trail, I bet that mutt could find her. Of course, that is, if you've got something with her scent on it. A dog can only do so much without a little bit of help."

Alabama grinned. Doc had given him Alice's drab gown. "We're prepared," he claimed.

The old man was tired and hobbled over to the chair and sat down. He coughed into his sleeve and then smacked his lips. "Sad is my fate," said the crumpled soldier. "I have no refuge from my past, and the friends I trusted are gone. Never again will we embrace one another or toast to days we believed in. But isn't it strange, where this cabin's door had led you and me? I am a weed in the field, but you have the potential to become a thistle."

"A thistle?" said Alabama. "Isn't that a weed too?"

The old soldier nodded, "Yes, but one with thorns. You must do something with your life, make it difficult for the occupiers. Thistles can be very beautiful and docile from a distance, but try to pick one, and you will find out just how assertive it is."

Alabama tried to visualize the field, and in his brain, he was balancing the metaphor with both admiration and perplexity. He looked at the bent-over fellow who carried his scarred face with bravery and took in the words.

"A soldier is a vagabond, like a wanderer of many lands. I have met, fought, and observed many people, so I feel qualified to give you advice." He stared with his weary eyes at the boy. "Most people are fearful of their troubles and wish for life to be easy. The natural trait of humankind is laziness, hiding behind their customs. Putting this all together, each person dreams of a utopian life where there is no suffering, only well-being. But, without the dread or expectation of fear, we would be merely like cows put out to pasture in the field and then brought back to the barn. Day in and day out. Such has become the life under the occupiers."

Inja pushed the open door with her nose and bounded into the room in her usual exuberant manner. She made several laps around the room until finally settling down by the feet of Alabama. The bent-over soldier placed his hands on his knees and pushed himself up. "I've enjoyed our talk," Alabama said. An overture for his departure.

"Well, I hope you find your friend," the soldier said. "If you think about what I said, then you might be alright. Remember that dogs have instinct; you have will."

The voice touched Alabama, and he felt obliged to say something witty; however, he wasn't very clever with words. "I wish I could give you something for your kindness," he said.

The old soldier smiled, and standing as erect as he could, he saluted. "Carry that with you, boy, and remember to honor your grandfather."

＊ ＊ ＊

The charges against Alabama Bailiwick satisfied the authorities thanks to the collective manipulation by Deputy Gris and Senior Deputy Khanna. The plan to apprehend the boy in the outer regions was accepted, allowing them to forgo further interrogations with Trenton Bailiwick. It had crossed their minds that the old man might have the whereabouts of his grandson;

the notion of him tipping off the boy to their tactic was not out of the question.

A rookie officer, Captain Bangkok, sat behind Gris's desk and stroked the wood, admiring its smooth finish. "You don't need to worry, Sir," he said, "I'll take care of everything in your absence."

"Don't get too comfortable, Bangkok," grunted the Deputy. "We won't be gone long." Though pleased to be out of the cramped office, Gris didn't like the idea of heading into the outer region. A suspicious man by nature, he lacked the comfort of his authority when in a territory notorious for renegades. However, he would keep silent on the subject, especially with Khanna, who considered himself a class above the rest. However, when the realization that an automobile would be too large to maneuver around the narrow paths, and each of them would have to ride a motorbike, Khanna secretly damned his entire plan. All dignity was lost as he envisioned his large posterior teetering on the small leather seat. His only salvation was knowing Gris was not a specimen of fitness. But, alas, they always did as ordered, regardless of how humiliating it was.

Chapter 22

*W*hy the mole, Father? What is so special about the mole? The mole is a survivor, he said. It lives beneath the ground, a rather difficult place to exist, don't you think? Alice could hardly disagree with him. Why don't they come up from the tunnel to make their homes? she asked. Because, he said, to be out in the open is to be vulnerable. Oh, said Alice, the mole is quite clever. Yes, the father said, quite clever indeed.

* * *

Building homes beneath the ground
His favorite game is hide and seek
Find him at the old mill creek
Travel at an easy pace
Until the stones are out of place

Mr. Paris was correct. The old mill creek resembled a barren landscape of sun-dried mud curled and pocked with tiny holes.

Beneath its crust was a treasure unknown to most, except the few birds and burrowers, a tell-tale of a once flourishing body of water. But Alice did not have a weak eye or a weak memory and knew she had arrived. The sunlight had broken through the clouds dying the clay purple like a stain of wine. She walked across what was once a natural waterway. Every now and again, the location of the curious habitation under the ground was revealed above by fairy rings. The cadence of her walk was slow and unhurried, and as Alice appraised her surroundings, she recited the rhyme. She needed to locate the stones, yet they would not necessarily be at the site of the fairy rings. Nevertheless, it all seemed rather straightforward to Alice. Follow the path starting at the mound nearest the end of the creek bed.

However, she did not anticipate that two paths were leading from the edge of mill creek into the frontier. They both were similar in physical appearance, yet after a short observation, one was somewhat narrower. *Suppose I'm unaware of the unawareness I could meet, then the decision to take the path I believe is correct may be the wrong path. But I am aware that there could be something I am unaware of, which returns me to my choices. So it is a dilemma since either path is right or wrong.* With that, Alice bent down and tugged on her shoelace, pulling it free. Then she tied it to a tall, sturdy weed with a bow in case she made a mistake, which she never did, so she could find her way back and begin again.

The desert-colored path of splintered rocks meandered away from mill creek. The terrain was changing with a wash of browns and greens, and as she walked, the trail took a steady climb upward. Taller shrubs grew undisturbed with increasing density, and for the first time, flowering weeds of yellow and pink adorned the landscape. A few stunted conifers grew in clumps like a miniature forest, and in all directions, green dominated the landscape. Tired from her morning travels, the youth decided to rest, settling alongside a clearing by the path. Though rocky and lacking shade, Alice found these prehistoric-looking boulders comforting. Just in view, she could see a structure, possibly of brick construction.

Travel at an easy pace

Until the stones are out of place

And so, she continued on.

* * *

It was already afternoon, and the faint outline of a crescent moon appeared overhead as Dakar Hamlet pushed her bike into the alleyway. The absence of regret surprised her as she opened her apartment door and shuddered with disgust to discover she was devoid of moral sense. "Even a dog regrets missing a bone tossed away by the butcher. Yet every choice comes with regret," Dakar mused.

The wine glass was on the table where she had left it. Everything was in place, and everything was out of place. Doc's face, such an evocative expression she had never seen, was revealed. Dakar pulled off her jacket and threw it on the chair.

She walked over to the window and raised the blinds. A grey shadow shaded the street. A lighted window at the apartment across the way glowed orange, a strange color for a light bulb. Or is it? Maybe it was just a way of looking at it. Beyond these walls, stretching toward nowhere and everywhere, an orange beam flickering from one flame, one bulb, and with one breath, you could blow it out. With one word, it's extinguished.

She opened the window and leaned out, hoping to get a peek inside the orange apartment. It was at that moment she had an incredible urge to go out. To go somewhere, anywhere. A need to leave arrived with a fury of unknowns, all of which flooded her head with questions. She could take the train; she hadn't been on one in ages. And go where? Everything she ever did had a purpose, and now that she felt a need to do something out of the ordinary, it was uncomfortable. As if she were putting on someone else's shoes. She turned and glanced around the apartment. A light breeze crept inside, reminding her to shut the window. It was not a complicated decision. She picked up her jacket and walked out.

* * *

Dakar Hamlet found herself standing in front of the National Museum, an enormous granite building; though having been neglected since the occupation, its grandeur still endured. She lifted her eyes to read the quote etched in stone above the portico. "Let all who enter leave with something new." A brutish-looking guard wearing a blue uniform and too-tight a matching cap looked at her credentials. "What is your intent?" he asked

"My intent?"

"Yes, Consociate Hamlet, what are your intentions after you get inside?"

Dakar looked at his face, but he wasn't laughing; he was serious. Her eyes passed his badge. "I am going to look around. Like those people leaving," she said, directing her attention away.

Officer Milan turned his head as a man and woman dressed in civilian clothes were hurrying down the steps. "Those two, they come to fraternize. She's the wife of one of the Admirals," he whispered. "So, I ask you again, if I let you pass, what are your intentions?"

"Perhaps I have made a mistake." Hamlet supposed. Her sincerity was genuine. It was possible this building was no longer a museum. "I thought this was the National Museum."

"It is. See," he said, pointing to the sign on the wall. It was becoming clear that the guard's patience was waning as he began to tap his foot with disapproval.

"I want to walk around and look at the art."

The guard looked down at her card. "To look at the art," he repeated.

"Yes, I suppose it might seem like an idle way to spend the afternoon, but then again, I might see something I didn't see before."

"And what might that be?" he questioned. "Do you think this is a garden and a new flower blooms every day?"

"You have a point," she agreed and sighed, thinking that she was possibly deceiving herself. "If you really must know, I'm looking for a color," Dakar admitted. "Orange, I saw this orange light in an apartment across from mine and just had to find out if it existed elsewhere. That's when I decided to come here. It just seemed logical."

Officer Milan fumbled with her credentials and let her pass after a moment of hesitation. "One hour, that is your allotment, one hour," he reminded her.

"Thank you, Officer," she smiled and slipped through the doorway.

Upon entering the Great Gallery, Dakar was greeted by strange allegorical figures raised on fluted pedestals. Marble sculptures missing arms and legs, some with chipped noses and broken garments. Elaborate carvings chiseled on stone slabs lined the walls like an ancient marble path. Dakar walked quickly, avoiding other visitors who stopped every few feet like buyers at a market. The purity of the marble did not strike her fancy, and she weaved around until she came upon a grand stairway with a vaulted ceiling leading into a picture gallery. A child stood beside a woman looking at an ornately framed painting. Neither of them noticed Dakar enter the room since the woman was busy explaining to the little girl the artist's intentions. The mother continued to prattle when suddenly the child pulled her hand free and began to skip about the woman as if she were a Maypole. The antics seemed rather strange until Dakar glanced at the painting. It was obvious the child was simply imitating art.

A clock above the straight rows of paintings was hanging on the wall by two hooks. Dakar hadn't thought much about it until she became conscious of the ticking. Like a warning tone, the noise gnawed at her nerves. The wheels inside the timekeeper were turning and turning, deleting time. Her heart, united with the clock, beat at the same pace. Yet the clock's ticking was not unique to this room, and as she walked through the passageway, fixed on the wall in a prominent location, was an equally annoying clock. This public time was infecting her personal time, Dakar thought, scorning the timepiece.

She glanced casually at the paintings. The same color blue of the sky, the same green of the trees, the colors were the same. The consumption of colors from artist to audience was the same. She refused to make eye contact with the subjects. Men, women, horses, and dogs, she passed all without eavesdropping into their conversations. She shrugged, listening to the clock; her pace hastened, almost jogging into the next room, a smaller version of the other galleries only square, not rectangular. She looked up and noticed a clock without a minute hand, broken and silent. The stillness was loud, and her breathing was louder. There were no other patrons; she was alone, face-to-face with a portrait set in a plain gold-leaf frame. Untouchable, it looked alive. Life squeezed from tubes of paint. There was dust on the frame. Dakar drew closer and slid her finger along the edge. The bird in the foreground was singing; Dakar was sure it was coming from the painting. But, no, the guard in the other room was whistling. He poked his head in, "Twenty minutes," he said. The clock without its hand mocked him.

The woman in the portrait was sitting in the shade. Her head tilted slightly; her brown hair tied back with an orange ribbon. Her lips faintly parted, the color of madness; not angry madness but a wild, untamed madness. Yet, the eyes, a stare fixed straight ahead, undisturbed. There was nothing fragile about the woman, nothing delicate or even demure; she was simply quite handsome, beautiful, and composed. Dakar closed her eyes, and as if her lids were a cork, she captured the image. With eyes shut, she could focus on just the face, like a square on a patchwork quilt, but with eyes open, the entire painting came into view. "Are we strangers?" whispered Dakar. The picture belonged to her. It spoke to her not in a superior tone but as an equal; the way she and Doc would talk. Dakar looked behind her, hoping no one was watching, and then she stepped forward and placed her hand on the painting. It was cold. She leaned closer, her cheek nearly grazing the canvas when she was startled by footsteps entering the gallery.

"Your time is up," commanded the guard. Dakar pulled back and looked up at the clock. Its timeless face locked in the moment. The triviality of the subject, a woman, sitting alone, filled her with melancholy; she saw something in herself which frightened her.

* * *

"You asked to see me, Sir?" The voice was of Officer Milan. He was standing in the open threshold with his cap in his hand. A moment elapsed until the man sitting behind the desk acknowledged him.

"Come in, come in," waved Captain Bangkok. "I've just been reading over your dispatch. There was an incident, I see." He looked up. "Come forward, man. How can I speak with you cowering in the doorway?"

Milan stepped forward, wondering why he had been summoned. The incident had been documented to the best of his recollection. "Isn't this Senior Deputy Khanna's desk? I was under the assumption I would be reporting to the Senior Deputy."

"He was called away on assignment. I'll be taking care of this inquiry."

"Inquiry, Sir?" Milan could feel his face growing flush.

"Just routine, Milan, nothing out of the ordinary. Unless you haven't included something we should know." His eyes glared with intimidation. A few seconds of silence fell. "The report says that Consociate Hamlet Dakar was in the painting gallery at the National Museum; she was sitting on the floor in front of one of the pictures. Sitting?" questioned the captain. "Isn't that rather odd?"

"That's what we thought, Guard Santiago and I."

"You reported that Santiago came by and reminded her it was time to leave, that her hour was up. But when Guard Santiago told her to leave, she refused and sat down." Bangkok leaned back in his chair and lifted the report. "That's when you walked into the gallery, reaffirmed her hour was up, but she still refused to leave peacefully. That's when Santiago began to approach Dakar, and she shouted, 'If you come any closer, I'll bite you!'"

"Exactly, Sir."

"So, Santiago was threatened by her teeth."

"I suppose you could say that. They are sharp, you know," Milan added.

"Then you explained that you would remove her by force if she did not leave immediately. When she didn't obey, you drew your firearm from your holster and pointed it at her."

"That is correct."

"Again, you reminded her of the consequences, and she exclaimed she didn't care. You tried to reason with her again, but she would not budge. It was now approaching ten minutes over the allotted time permitted in the Museum, and as you noted, you were within your rights to remove her by any means." Milan nodded in agreement to the report. He could feel the sweat on his brow trickling down the sides of his face. "You warned her one more time; that's when she shouted, 'Aim at me, not her!' An instant followed, and you fired."

"That's correct, Sir."

"You waited a moment and then called for help to remove the body. That's when you went into the Museum office and wrote up the report."

"Yes," Milan agreed. A sense of calm suddenly passed over him. He wondered if he might get a promotion.

"And the painting; I checked, and it was a portrait commissioned before the occupation." Captain Bangkok slid the paper aside and smiled. "All in a day's work, Milan. Why don't you go home and have a stiff drink."

"I will, Sir, but there's just one thing if I may speak off the record. I could swear she wanted me to shoot her. There was something regretful in the way she looked. I didn't write it down, but I think her last word was Doc."

Part VI

Where the path leads

Chapter 23

Nebraska awoke at the same time each night, leading the boy to believe it was an omen, but of what, he didn't know. He pulled his covers to his chin and turned his head towards his brother's empty cot. Since Alabama's departure, the bedroom hadn't changed, and Nebraska vowed not to move anything out of order. His thoughts ferried back and forth, wondering when Alabama would return, thoughts that kept him stirring until eventually, he fell back to sleep.

* * *

"It's time we talked," the old man said. He pushed his plate aside and pulled the coffee cup towards him. Although it was cold by now, he didn't care. He liked coffee and was used to drinking it any way it was served, black, creamed, sugared, hot, cold, but not weak. That's where the old man drew the line.

Nebraska was used to their talks, but the tone in the man's voice seemed more like a demand than a discourse. He looked up. "Okay," he said. "What about?" He supposed with winter approaching, he would get a reminder about having to search farther into the outlands to gather seeds. Collecting seeds was always on the old man's mind. But it was not about seeds.

"Searching for wisdom can take a lifetime, and most of the people you'll meet are either dreamers or followers, none of whose consequences will offer advice. It's okay to be a lone cat among a pack of dogs, but you must be able to conduct yourself within their culture; otherwise, they will consume you." The old man picked up his coffee cup and took a drink. Then he settled it down on the table, not the saucer. Nebraska felt a sudden dread but remained suspiciously quiet, which the old man took as fear.

"What about Alabama? When will he get home?"

"Are you worried he'll be eaten?" the grandfather asked.

"I don't know." His voice drifted with worry as the words were no longer obscure. He agreed and denied without facts. "I don't even know where he is, yes," Nebraska exclaimed, "he's out there, somewhere, and no one will tell me where." The boldness in his youthful voice gave the elder reason for hope. Nebraska always listened to his brother; like the wind that pushes the sail, so did Alabama move Nebraska through life. It wasn't always the right way, but it worked. The old man's mouth didn't move, and the boy waited for him to speak. "Where is he, Grandpa?"

"I don't know, I did know, but now I don't. He went in search of the girl, Alice. He's in the frontier, and that's all I know."

Nebraska sighed and then gritted his teeth. He bowed his head; he was angry, sad, and bitter. "Is this why you want to talk about Alabama?" He wiped his eyes with his napkin.

"No, not on account of Alabama. On account that you need your own talk. You're a good boy, Nebraska. We might never see your brother again, we may never know where he ends up, but he's on his own journey. Alice is a smart girl. He'll be all right."

"How do you know?"

Such a question needed an answer. "Because he's part of you and me, that's how come I know." The response satisfied the questioning boy. "Alabama may be a good-for-nothing, but he's got sense. Good Bailiwick sense. You have the same sense; it just needs to be improved." The old man laughed, lightening the boy's hurt. Nebraska was at the age when action precluded thinking. He was a runaway colt that needed to be bridled. Trenton lifted the coffee cup and drained what little remained.

"Do you want more?" Nebraska began to get up from the table to retrieve the pot. The old man waved his hand no. There was a sputtering in the grandfather's head, words and feelings interrupting his thoughts. He closed his eyes and exhaled. His face wore the expression of wisdom.

"Before the time of humanity, when only animals roamed the earth, all the animals were friends. The cat liked the dog, the wolf liked the sheep, and the fox liked the lemmings. As if one big family, they agreed to be harmonious. If one animal had nothing to eat, the other would share. That is the way it was for many years. That is until a bird, the seagull, returned with news of an undiscovered land. 'Here,' said the gull, 'all the animals live in luxury. They have enormous nests and enormous caves and can eat as much as they want.'

'So do we,' said the animals.

'Except,' said the seagull, some animals have more than others, so they can live with more luxury.' Then she flew away.

That evening the fox, who had been present at the gull's speech, wondered why the animals in the undiscovered land were able to have more finery. So, he took it upon himself to find out. That night, when all the other animals slept, he crept to the seagull's nest and woke her up. 'In the undiscovered land, why do some of the animals have more?' the fox asked.

The seagull turned over in her nest and opened her eyes. 'That is easy,' she replied. 'There are more of them, so they get more.' Then she fell back to sleep.

For several days the fox thought about what the seagull told him, and for several days he complained that there wasn't enough food. Soon the wolf heard him, and so did the dog. They all complained, growing greedier and stingier. Soon the wolf was hungry all the time, and so was the fox, and so was the dog, so they agreed upon a plot. If we get rid of one of the animals, there will be more for us, but which one.

So, they decided to wait until evening to ask the wisest of the animals, the owl. The owl was sitting on her perch when they approached. Since she was very wise, the owl did not come down but listened from the limb of the oak tree she was sitting on. And after they told their tale of being hungry all the time and wondering which animal was taking most of the food, the owl thought. The moon came up, and the three villains waited.

Finally, she spoke. 'It seems to me that the lemmings and the mice are eating the most.' And then she flew away.

After the moon rose and the stars came out, the fox spoke up. 'Since I am the hungriest, I will take it upon myself to rid us of the lemmings. Leave it to me.'

The following day, he went to the meadowlands where the lemmings were sunning themselves and welcomed the fox readily. 'What a fine surprise,' Mr. Lemming said. 'How are you this fine morning?'

'Not very well, that's why I am here!' exclaimed the fox. 'I was hoping you could help me. I have heard you are fine swimmers, and one of my children has fallen over the cliff. Could you come and help?'

'Ah,' said the lemming, 'we would like to help you, but this body of water, is it a river or the ocean?'

'What will happen if it is the ocean?' asked the fox, talking with his most understanding voice.

'We may drown,' said the lemming.

'Nonsense!' exclaimed the fox. 'You lemmings are known for your excellent abilities; you can swim better than most fish!' Charmed by the fox's flattery, all the lemmings gathered round. Then, heartened by what they had heard, they followed the fox to the edge of the cliff. Below, the waves hit the rocky shore and blew the foamy crests. 'Down there,' pointed the fox, 'I know how great you are, like waterfowl only with beautiful brown fur. 'Jump!' cried the devious fellow. 'Jump!'

The next day the fox, the dog, and the wolf were enjoying the meal set aside for the lemmings. They had eaten all the food the lemmings had stored away for the winter and still greedy set out to find the mice." The old man looked grave and searched Nebraska for a sign of understanding.

"Did you make up that story?" Nebraska asked.

"In a way, yes. There's a myth about lemmings rushing head-long over a cliff that traces back before my time, but the reason I told you the story is because its meaning needs to be interpreted. What is not told is of the greatest importance. All the characters in the story are animals, but let's pretend the characters were not animals but instead people. If that was the case, then the story could explain the way people behave and interact with one another." Nebraska forgot his gloomy mood as he leaned forward, taking the challenge. "Let's start with the animals in the beginning; who could they be?"

"Oh, that's easy, you said in the beginning. If they were all the animals, then they would be all the people," the boy implored with success in his answer.

"A point for you!" exclaimed the old man. "Let's get to the seagull."

Nebraska thought for a mere moment. "No one special, except someone that might want an adventure."

"True, that would be possible; it certainly seems so," the elder agreed. "Now the fox, the wolf, and the dog, what about them? But before you answer, I want you to try to raise the level and think specifically."

"They were cruel," Nebraska said.

"Yes, quite cruel," Trenton agreed.

But after a few moments, he declared himself defeated. "I don't know anyone that mean," the boy announced.

"Perhaps we should narrow your thinking. We'll think of the three animals as a type of group. Does that help?"

Suddenly the boy's eyes widened, and his mouth was agape. Then, in a hushed voice, he offered his guess. "The occupiers, they're the occupiers."

"And the owl? This is a hard one; maybe I should give you a hint," suggested Trenton. "Who would the occupiers get help from?"

"Another occupier!" shouted Nebraska.

"Exactly, and since the owl represented someone that was supposed to be wise, we can say maybe it would be a judge. And the lemmings, who are the lemmings?" asked the grandfather.

It was apparent now that the boy had no doubt in his mind. "They're the citizens," he blurted, "the citizens!"

"Good job, Nebraska!" encouraged the old man. However, despite the boy's grasp, the core of the story needed to be unraveled. Trenton stood up and poured himself more coffee. "Want some?" he asked the boy as he pulled another cup off the shelf.

"Me, coffee?" The remark seemed incredulous.

"Sure, a cup won't hurt. I'll add some milk and sugar. You've shown you're old enough to enjoy a cup with your old Grandpa." Delighted by the aspect, Nebraska watched as the old man set his cup on the table. He had always wanted to try but knew it was strictly out of the question. He blew over the rim and slurped. "What do you think, like it?"

"Good, not bad, but I think a little more sugar might help."

The morning was satisfying, and though the mood was peaceful, Trenton needed to continue. "So, I was wondering about the story. There's a puzzle piece that needs some deciphering. Are you game?"

Nebraska stopped stirring the added sugar and set the spoon down to listen. "Okay, let me try."

"It goes back to the lemmings. Why did they listen to the fox when he told them all to jump over the cliff?"

Nebraska fell silent. His mind thought of Alabama and wondered if his brother could answer the question more quickly. He imagined the lemmings and then the fox with its long bushy tail and beady-eyed, and suddenly an answer bubbled to the top. "They trusted him, Grandpa."

"That's right, Nebraska; they trusted him." *There were a million things he wanted to tell the boy. He wanted to explain how they got to the place they were in. How, after Blank, chaos ensued around the world, opening the gates to demagogues, dictators, and the occupation. He wanted him to understand it was popular opinion that usurped truth. Intimidation, corruption, and false narratives brought people into a condition that they were willing to be soldiers and followers. The original Representative Government was motivated by personal gain rather than the public good, making it highly corruptible. He wanted him to realize true leaders can bring order out of turmoil and reconcile the order for their people. But now it was too late. He wanted Nebraska to know this is how we got here, but all that information was too much for a boy having his first cup of coffee.*

Trenton's head sputtered until he parceled his words to meet the listener. "What should the lemmings have done? What should people do?" Trenton reflected on his questions. If only he could have conveyed the answer fifty years ago, but he didn't. He sighed with dissatisfaction. However, at this moment, his ability to explain was more critical than ever. "Rhetoric," he continued. "It's the art of using language to persuade others, and unfortunately, rhetoric serves the purpose of the occupying authority. When the occupiers talk, they use flattery. And," added the old man, "they purposely mislead us by lying, sweet-talking, and pandering. This, my boy, is why you must learn to listen for language that distills principles and knowledge. The imperfect world we live in has become corrupted because the occupied citizens are gullible. A person may know justice but not be just. If the lemmings had believed in themselves, they might have been able to save themselves."

Chapter 24

It was Inja that set the boy on the correct path and a voice in his head echoing, *Find him at the old mill creek.* Alabama looked out from the dusty shore as if expecting water to roll over his feet. But it was only a few clouds that curled round the sun, greying the expanse before him. He could feel Alice's presence, a veil lifting yet not quite ready to remove the shroud of absence. *Travel at an easy pace, Until the stones are out of place.* The mud cracked like a peach pit. Inja led him across the grey terrain, every so often stopping to sniff. An impression made by a foot? The imagination conjures up what we want or what we fear. Alabama believed it belonged to Alice, bringing him closer to finding her. The path strayed in two directions, but unlike Alice, his preponderance for certainty lacked any logic. He left the decision to instinct, not his, but Inja's.

* * *

Deputy Gris lowered his kickstand and stretched. Senior Deputy Khanna was smoking a cigarette and laughed mockingly as the man approached. "What's so funny?" Gris asked, but he already knew without being told. His posterior was not used to such a hard seat, and he walked with more than discomfort. He was sore.

"You, you're what's so funny," the superior officer said. A cigarette buried between his thumb and index finger was flicked. "Sun's so hot it melted the clouds."

Gris nodded with agreement loitering in the shade of a boulder. "Are you ready to have something to eat?" Khanna asked. He glanced around. "I suppose this is as good a place as any," and eyeing the miserly bit of shade, he removed a bag of sandwiches and canteen of water from his saddlebag. Complaining about the accommodations would do no good, so Deputy Gris gingerly sat down and leaned against the boulder.

He released a heavy sigh which immediately agitated Khanna. "Now what?"

Gris stopped mid-way into biting his jam sandwich and looked up. "Nothing," he said.

"Well, there must be something; I heard you groan," protested Khanna. "So, what is it?"

"I just never liked going into the frontier, that's all."

Although the words sounded like a premonition, Khanna didn't answer and kept eating. He mulled the statement over. "I wouldn't worry; we have our pistols."

"Our pistols? You have a pistol?" Gris questioned.

The unfortunate thing about conversations can be the order of the words, the words in the sentence, and the way it's delivered. Even if the receiver inverted them, such as, 'Have you a pistol?' the same message pointed to the original analysis. Khanna gestured with his sandwich. "You're in charge of sidearms. I put them in your saddlebag."

"What saddlebag?" asked Gris.

"The saddlebag on your desk. I placed it there myself!" Khanna hollered. "You idiot! Are you sure?"

Gris wondered how long the man would protest before realizing that the saddlebag was still in the office. He would know if it was on his motorbike. Gris ate the rest of his sandwich and watched Khanna as he lumbered over to the motorbike. The portly man raised his hands overhead and then slapped his sides. There was a shake of the head and a loud expletive. Moments turned to minutes, and in a half-an-hour, they rode away.

* * *

Travel at an easy pace, Until the stones are out of place, Look to the east and down split logs, Part the reeds to see the frogs, Follow the mole where the old creek falls, And red vines climb over stony-walls. Alice continued eastward, but there were no logs or reeds. The simple rhyme written long ago did not know the earth would change from wet to dry. It would not have known the frogs would no longer be present. So far, the only tell-tale traces were stones too heavy to be taken by scavengers, and only someone searching for these clues would notice them. Alice removed her compass and aligned her sites using the stand of trees in the distance. The vine-covered wall would be concealed by foliage; everything her parents ever did was masked in secrecy. This was a constant she could rely on. It was most probable the wall was not very far off.

"Are you afraid, Alice?" It was Atlantis.

Alice scowled. "I thought I left you back with the girls," she scolded. "But since you ask, no, I'm not afraid. So, why are you here?"

"I was afraid," Atlantis confessed.

"Of what?"

"Don't think I'm silly, but without you, I was afraid I would become nothing. Everything I know is because of you. Without you, I'm not anything," simpered the alter-ego. "I felt myself dissolving away."

"Well, how do you know I'll find what I'm looking for, suppose I needed to come back to you?" asked Alice, a bit annoyed.

"At least you're heading somewhere. Anyway, maybe I can help you," Atlantis said in her most convincing voice.

"You do have a point," Alice agreed. "Your evaporation would be like time and water and losing both is a shame."

"Then I can stay!" exclaimed the alter-ego.

But without replying, Alice shooed Atlantis to the back of her mind with anticipation of finding the wall before nightfall. But she was glad not to be alone. Atlantis was like her snowflake; they were made of the exact same substance sharing the same shadow, yet she was different. The wall beyond her reach was an insignificant destination to most, and the most meaningful of journey's end for Alice. There was no more to the rhyme, *Follow the mole where the old creek falls, And red vines climb over stony-walls.*

* * *

Alabama did not notice the shoelace Alice had tied to the weed and walked right past the very spot she attached it to. But the trailing officers traversing the same path drove headlong into the same area where Senior Officer Khanna spotted the marked foliage. He stopped only for a moment before waving his companion on to follow. He was unaware of the owner; however, after examining the lace, he suspected it had been exposed to the elements for only a short time. Whoever attached it could not be far ahead. And, by the length of the lace, it belonged to someone younger than an adult. Khanna grinned. It would not be long before he met up with the boy.

* * *

The old veteran backtracked when he heard the unfamiliar sound of motored vehicles, the reminiscent sensation of danger. He hid in the brush. The low branches shielded him from the approaching riders, and as he waited, the bad blood he felt towards the occupiers resurfaced. Only the authorities would be so full of bravado to make their presence in the frontier so obvious. The motorbikes approaching offered the old soldier time to decide what to do. He could remain hidden or find out what they were up to. Pulling the bush out of his way, he walked out and looked across the vacant space, sizing up the path. The noisy sounds of sputtering and clatter swelled, drawing closer until he was standing in front of the approaching officers. Gris shouted in a brassy voice for him to move aside. But the old soldier pretended not to hear, and with his head bowed, he strode forward without adhering to the demand. Once again, there was a shout that his presence prevented their ability to continue on the path. "You, old man, what are you doing?" Senior Officer Khanna shouted, stopping his motorbike abruptly.

The old soldier's eyes wandered upward onto the stony face. "I was going to ask you the same," said the veteran. His rumpled uniform made him look more disheveled than usual, and the duffle bag he was carrying weighted him over on his right side. "I'm walking," he said, "no law against that."

"Well, no, but in the middle of the road is!" shouted the officer.

The veteran looked up and then down, to the left and then to the right. "Road? This is a path, a walking path. Seems that you're the ones breaking the law," he said.

"Why you impertinent old fool," exclaimed Officer Gris, coming to the defense of his superior. "I could arrest you on the spot."

The old man glared defiantly, "I imagine you could," he replied.

"But we're in a hurry; otherwise, we would," Khanna said. "We're on official business looking for a delinquent who's been seen in this vicinity."

The old soldier took off his cap and wiped the sweat from his forehead. "Only one?" he asked slyly. "Aren't you both out of your comfort zone here in the frontier," the old man toyed. "But to answer your question, I might, and then I might not have. What did you say this delinquent did?"

Gris turned to Khanna and then shrugged as if to admit he wasn't really sure. "That, old fool, is not your business." Khanna straddled the motorbike and revived the engine with impatience. "Have you or have you not seen the boy?"

"Oh, it's a boy you're looking for. Why didn't you say so? I think I may have seen one around, but I have a bad memory. Sometimes I forget things. But if you go slowly, there may be some prints around," the soldier confessed and stepped away from blocking the path. An unfamiliar bloom on a strangling vine smelled sweet with a fragrance he couldn't identify.

Khanna appeared disgusted but took the man's suggestion seriously. The two officers started on again without fanfare, straddling the motorbikes to keep their balance as they searched for prints. The old soldier hobbled back into the bush and retrieved his rifle in less than a minute. The pair had not made it too far down the path when he lifted the firearm and steadied it against his shoulder. He obeyed his instinct to defend the boy. "Turn and meet your maker!" the old vet shouted. The wind carried his voice. Khanna turned first and looked full face into the man behind the barrel. He opened his mouth, but the blast of the rifle deafened the angry denial. A second shot was fired as Gris cursed his destiny. Both men slumped forward as their motorbikes careened into the brush, making their departures from the scene a most convenient death.

Chapter 25

This was her life, and it was simple. "Simple does not mean easy," Atlantis reminded Alice. But the youth ignored the alter-ego, who sometimes complained unnecessarily. Alice found herself standing on the path, looking up at a clear, cloudless, and birdless sky. On her journey, she would scatter seeds on the ground. Her imminent arrival was the culmination of her parents' formidable plan. Yet the uncomfortable truth yielded one vital component. When she arrived, it might be the end, and if it is the end, time will not pass anymore. What would she do with all the time accumulating? She certainly couldn't scatter it about willy-nilly. It would have to be weighed and measured, and set somewhere. "Perhaps," Alice thought, "it would evaporate. Or maybe, when I arrive, it won't be the end but the beginning." She was glad Atlantis was sleeping because she couldn't bear to explain this all over again.

The path's surface was becoming uneven from the numerous roots of old trees that rolled up above the soil, making it necessary to continue with caution. Where to find an entrance to this wilderness of broken rock? It seemed possible now that the crumbling wall in the distance spanned a greater length and height than at first glance. Built with security in mind, it was cloistered behind a stand of trees. One tall trunk had been shattered by lightning, its branches charred and gnarled pointed upward. Like moles that build tunnels and chambers, horrendous disturbances on the surface forced refuge seekers underground. If only the shrubs and vines hiding this underground world would slowly part, for it was their thick leaves, stems, and tendrils keeping her from accomplishing her tasks. Alice gazed ahead; the light faded away on fragmented walls, leaving a hazy purple tint. Rocks bleached grey and steely, except where moss fringed the mortar yielded nothing out of the ordinary to the naked eye but to the ear; Alice could hear rustling in the fallen leaves. The youth turned around with a mixture of curiosity and dread. She could not see anyone, but the figure could see her. A strange feeling washed over her as she rounded a curve in the path. Emerging from the shadows, as if having been quarried from marble, the cunning dog scampered to her side. The moon had risen in the daylight, pairing with a cloud.

"This is where dreams are made," Alabama said, falling behind the dog.

"You're here," said Alice, her eyes fixed upon his face. "You shouldn't be here." *Why'd you say that? whispered Atlantis.* But Alice tossed her to the back of her mind. Inja scampered freely; her job was complete, having found the girl. "It's just that you're not safe wandering around, especially here," Alice warned.

"Either are you," exclaimed Alabama. He was tired and burdened with concern. "You're hard to keep up with. I've been trailing you for days. If it weren't for Inja, I would never have found you." The dog, hearing her name, romped back to Alabama and waited for attention. But Alabama was too distracted to take notice of the dog. A compromise of silence between the boy and the girl, a language they understood, erased any doubt of their feelings. What they had gathered between them was parceled out in the shape of mute gratitude. Inja led with her nose to the ground. They walked together; heads bowed as if on sacred land. "Did you find what you're looking for?"

"Looking for?" Alice asked in a dreamy voice.

"Yes, the moles, the fairy rings."

"Well, yes and no. This is the correct location, but not the right spot." Her answer was purposely vague. The day had grown, drawing out as much light as possible like a candle burning down. Twilight was removing small patches of blue sky, gradually exchanging it for fuchsia. "The trees are generous with their leaves," she said. "If we pile some up against the stones, we can rest."

"You don't mind sleeping out in the open?" Alabama asked, looking around for a bit of shelter.

"We won't be in the open," Alice remarked. "Look, up; soon we'll be under a blanket of stars. We're lucky; most are sent to bed when the stars come out. It seems night hides things, but in fact, it is we who hide."

So, the boy and girl gathered leaves and put them in piles against the stones while the dog snooped about finding sticks and twigs. Dusk's sluggish beginning unceremoniously ended as they stretched Alice's blanket on the ground, and the dog sat between them. Fate had reserved this night, setting the stars and moon in harmony. Patches of moonlight roamed freely like a pale river. Alabama removed a cloth napkin from his sack and offered Alice a handful of crushed acorns and wild chives. "I've got some bread and dried meat for Inja in here too. But I remember you liked the seeds," he said, smiling cunningly.

"Atlantis thought that was pretty funny," she exclaimed and pinched a bit between her fingers. He watched as she ate it and nodded approvingly. "Not bad, a little spicy, but pretty good."

"And what does Alice think?" he asked jokingly.

"I think it's quite different, good and spicy. However, I have something you might like." Looking in her bag, Alice rummaged the contents and removed two wrapped bars. "Here," she said, handing one to Alabama.

He watched as Alice unwrapped her bar and broke off a piece before eating. He followed her movement and did the same. "This is amazing!" he said. "What is it?"

"A protein bar. It's made with peanuts and raspberry, but I think the best part is the chocolate."

Alabama fumbled with the paper. "And what's this wrapping?"

"Cellophane, I think."

"Cellophane?" repeated Alabama. He looked up timidly and finished his bar, not admitting he had never seen nor heard of this wrapper she called cellophane. He tugged on it lightly and then balled it up and stuck it in his pocket.

"We'll save the dried meat for Inja," Alice said. "I'm not sure if the bar is good for dogs. I have lots of them in my bag. I've had them forever," she laughed. Forever, such a non-descript word, depending upon your frame of reference. To Alabama the word forever was now, a time that would and could not be lost, a time he would keep always.

"The sky is just one big map," Alice said, stretching out on the blanket. "Just attach a moonbeam thread from star to star, and you can draw a picture." Inja was already lying down, and the light rhythm of her breathing signaled she was asleep. Alabama leaned back on his elbows and tilted his head. "Trace an imaginary line from the North Star downward, and you should be able to find the two stars at the end of the Big Dipper's handle," Alice said. Alabama stared into the stars, thwarted by the complexity of what was before him. "There," she pointed, "the North Star is usually very bright; she's called Polaris."

"Polaris," Alabama repeated with uncertainty.

"Look north about one-third of the way from the horizon to the top of the sky. Now do you see it?" The sky loomed as if he were searching for a beacon while trying to stand on a rocking ship. "Count seven bright stars that point to the Polar Star, Polaris," Alice explained. "Then, attach them with an imaginary string; they make the Big Dipper."

"I'm afraid I've never heard of anything you're talking about," Alabama said gloomily.

"Reach up, and I'll guide your hand," and he listened while Alice steered him from star to star. "I always think of a clothesline and hanging out the stars," Alice mocked. Nothing but eyes and fingers grazed the mosaic heavens.

"There!" he exclaimed. "I see something, but it's not a dipper. It's a plow."

A plow? whispered Atlantis. That's what I heard too, Alice whispered back. "A plow?" repeated Alice aloud. "I guess it could be a plow and a dipper, depending upon who you ask," though not convinced with his answer, Alice could only assume they were looking at the same position of stars.

"How do you know so many things?" Alabama asked and lay on his back with his hand resting on Inja. The world was pocked with starlight. He felt quite small.

"You know the same as I do; you just don't see it," she said. "It's all here and there, up and down, a puzzle some have unraveled before others. The big dipper has forever been in the sky. Such ordinary objects lose their meaning until encountered. You just never let it show itself."

Alabama circled the sky over and over as tireless as the wind. His mind was a restless beehive as he perused the high dome of stars. But by now, Alice had fallen asleep beneath a diamond coronet.

* * *

Suppose every morning started with the same splendid sunrise, extinguishing the pink hues, and filling the gaps with blue. Tedium would set in. That's why we have grey clouds and overcast skies, so we can appreciate the things we take for granted and disentangle assumptions.

* * *

Alabama awoke with wonder. Not a curiosity or fascination, but an unwilled willingness to experience strangeness in the familiar. Last night's journey roused his senses, forgetting his preoccupations. Before, he was defined by things and people's actions, but now he had something utterly fantastic, a projection of possibilities and ambiguities. He had no comparisons for what he experienced.

Alice walked with Inja, following like the wake of a ship. "We went for water," she said, handing Alabama a full canteen. "I hope you don't mind, but I took yours too."

"We'd you get water?"

She pointed behind her, "at the spring not too far from here. If there are fairy rings, there's water," she explained. She sat down on the blanket and set her bag before her, removing two wrapped bars. "Breakfast," she smiled.

"Pleasure seems to follow her," Alabama thought. A cloud arched, bending over the sun. Before and behind them, the path's growth continued with the fulness of nature. Alice ate her breakfast lazily, unfettered by the unknown consequences of the day. Still, as quietly as the morning started, the natural order of things bracketed with tranquility was severed by Inja's barking. Walking out of the brush, the old veteran armed with a rifle showed himself.

"Inja girl," the elder exclaimed, greeting the dog gently, "don't you recognize me?" Inja raised her stance at the sound of the voice and, trotting over to Alabama, nudged the boy with her whining. The old veteran walked out into the open. He leaned on the butt of the rifle and commenced to speak. "I thought I'd find you eventually. You didn't leave much of a trail, except for the shoelace back a ways," he laughed.

"That was me," Alice said. *I Told you it was too obvious, complained Atlantis. You weren't even around when I tied it to the weed, scolded Alice. Go away!* "Did you have your breakfast," Alice asked. "We're having protein bars."

The old man scowled. "If it's granola, my teeth can't chew that stuff. I have old teeth."

Alice handed him a bar, "this one is just fruit and chocolate." He nodded with appreciation and put it in his pocket. "For later," he confessed. "Mind if I sit here on this stump, we can talk." He lowered himself down and placed his gun between himself and his feet. His elbows rested on his knees, and after removing his hat, he wiped his brow with his sleeve. "Tombstones are rock," he said. "These broken walls remind me of tombstones. You can lie down and sleep on some comfortably, as long as it isn't your own." He winked and then reached into his pocket and unwrapped his bar. *What's he talking about? Atlantis asked. But Alice didn't know so she didn't answer her.*

"Do you like it?" Alabama asked.

"Yes, this one tastes pretty good." The old man put half his bar back into his pocket and took his time chewing.

"You've eaten this before?" the boy wondered aloud.

"Well, not this exact flavor, but a bar similar. I haven't tasted one in a long while. Could even be decades." The old soldier brushed the ground with his foot. "Hard to find things in the frontier when there's so much growth. Take these leaves," he remarked, picking up a handful. "it's like looking for something in sand. The land is full of things that are lost."

"Oh, I haven't lost anything," Alice said. "I just can't find something."

The old man nodded. "And you, Alabama, you lost or just looking?"

The first sharp jab of indecision pricked Alabama. "I'm helping Alice," he said.

"Then you're looking," the veteran corrected. "And I guess Inja is helping too." The veteran stretched his legs out towards the blanket. "Don't mind me," he said, "I get kind of stiff." Inja returned with a stick and placed it by the elder's feet. "Thank you, just what I needed," he said. He pushed aside the leaves before him and, taking the stick, dragged the pointed end into the dirt. "This is the frontier, and we are here," he explained, scratching an X in the ground. "From what you have told me, Alice is attempting to locate a specific place; on the other hand, the exact location is purposely concealed, making it a secret to only those who know the precise location."

"And why do you think it's a secret?" Alabama asked.

"Because I have encountered wayfarers on the same path," the old veteran said.

"So, you know where it is," exclaimed the boy and looked at Alice with a smile.

"He didn't say he knew; he only said he encountered others," replied Alice.

As if playing a poker hand, the old veteran remained expressionless. "Look around," he said, waving the stick side-to-side. "The frontier resembles a tangled web, disjointed shrubs and trees; they make it very difficult when you're also confronted by a region which is temporally and spatially constrained by time. The wayfarers I met didn't have a map to direct one point to another. But traveling as a wayfarer means figuring out changes in an emerging land. You must assemble new intellect, not rearrange what you already know." The old veteran removed the protein bar from its wrapping and ate the leftover piece. "There's no monotony in this region," he claimed. Neither the boy nor the girl could disagree with the old man. The frontier was speckled with brown toadstools sprouting on untrodden moss when unexpectedly a new transformation takes over, and the root-bound path is aligned with a furry grove of lemongrass.

Alice drew a big arc with her hand. "I'm at all the junctions of wrong turns," she sighed. "My information is correct, and the place where I am to go remains obscure because, as you infer, the words, the lines of the words, backward or forwards, aloud or silent, are finite. The limit of my language defines the limit of my search. There is another piece," Alice mused.

Alabama's understanding grasped only a fraction of the chatter he heard. Perhaps Inja sensed his feelings, for the dog wedged itself between the boy and Alice. "What missing piece?" he asked.

"It's not missing," Alice said. "I was just never given any more than I have." She liked the boy and wished him not to worry. She leaned over and patted his arm.

Alabama had roamed, moving along the frontier with Inja. By the dry shores of the Old Mill Creek, he knew he had to find Alice. He had a responsibility, and though she was a stranger in the occupied country, she had done more good than most. The old veteran brought an altered condition of things to follow. The remaining moment trespassed with uncertainty. "Doubt wasn't there before," Alabama thought. Last night he was beginning to know who he was, but now he had to negotiate. "So now what?" he dared ask.

If you don't have all the pieces, you'll have to go back, Atlantis whispered. "I guess I'll have to go back," Alice parroted aloud.

The old man gestured to the girl. Slowly he raised his stiff old legs and stood up. "Listen, Alice, I hear the wind talking."

The ivy creeps on walls so old
It makes a trail green as mold
Heaped in piles stones lie in rest
Where birds and squirrels make their nests
Parting sunbeams to stairs once sealed
Count ten stones the way revealed

Chapter 26

The boy and the girl stood under a pale sky. Time marked not by hours but by moments drifting unmoored. The region leads them around a contour of arcs and spirals, guided by contorted hands made of vines. A path colored in shades of greens and browns rinses shadows away with sunshine. On everything, there is a scent of the unknown, smelling of premonitions. Then, the morning mutinied against the old man's rhetoric.

"What do you mean?" Alice protested. Things were turned inside out. She could hear an echo in her head of Atlantis asking the same thing. The question broke all the splendor, and she realized the desolate reality. Alabama questioned the same concern, and she hoped the response he would receive might differ from her own.

The old man's rumpled uniform made him appear tired. He raised his grey eyes and waited for a few seconds before speaking. "Alice is the past, Alabama is the future, and the present never exists since the mind roams back and forth between the two. Alice the historian, Alabama the political future; where she is going would alter all things set before you. Alabama does not know where he is going, and that is his storm to tame. As for Alice, she must continue alone on her journey. That is her destiny. You are on two different planes in the same world, both headed towards the future but at different speeds. For either one of you to change courses would be disastrous. You see, Alice knows too much. She has knowledge nobody yet knows." The old man had enough of talking and excused himself. "Come along, Inja, let's walk." And so the dog obeyed.

The old man's summation spread itself out like a thick dark fog, grey and cold. If words could smother embers of hope, so were these capable of extinguishing a dying sunset. "I'm confused," Alabama said. The man and the dog moved between the labyrinth of shrubs and trees. He watched as they maneuvered in unperturbed solitude. He marveled their indifference.

Why is he confused? Atlantis asked. It's pretty obvious. Shhh, you're not helping, go away! demanded Alice. A sad silence was all around them. "I imagine you're wondering about this," Alice said. She lowered her collar and exposed the blue tattoo. Alabama blinked. He hadn't dared ask, though imagined it had something to do with her past.

"Doc has one too," he said.

"One of these!" exclaimed Alice. The boy nodded.

"I don't have to know about it unless it has to do with why we can't be together." He lowered his eyes and picked up a red leaf. "Pretty, isn't it? Funny, every leaf looks the same until you stop and examine it. See," he said. "The lines go all the way up the center but barely reach the jagged edge. Very unique, like you, Alice."

"I was born long before you. Before Blank, I'm a newcomer," she said.

"Before Blank?" He was astounded.

"Yes, and that's all I should say. It's dangerous for you if I say anymore."

"I had a feeling it might be something like that. Everything about you is a mystery, but a good mystery because you're different, you are good. I want to be with you, Alice, I want to learn things from you."

Alice felt Atlantis squirming. Or perhaps, she thought, it wasn't Atlantis. What tied the boy and her together without a trace of twine? Was it the sunshine on the path or dandelions in tin cups? "It won't work," Alice said. "Our lives are unfolding into the future. We were given a chance to break in, and for a few moments, be together. But, if we don't go our own ways, I will demystify your world by revealing things to you that you can't know. I'm afraid I'll make it impossible for you to become who you're meant to be." Alice recognized an uncaging of feelings. "For awhile, I could believe in everything," she said.

"And I don't want to say goodbye," lamented Alabama.

"I wish you could go with me; I wish many things. But where I'm going doesn't even have an address," Alice laughed. "How would you let your grandfather or brother know where you were?"

"Well, if you can predict the future, can you tell me one thing?"

"I didn't say predict; I only said I knew." *Now you've really confused him, exclaimed Atlantis.* "It's hard to ask the right question when what you are seeking is not," the youth told him.

"Not what?" asked the boy.

"Not possible," answered Alice. She held out her hand, and he gently took it into his.

"You will always be around me," he said.

"That's how the past is; you can think about it with clarity, not like the future, a jumbled roll of what-ifs. I rather like thinking of myself as something you can define as real. So you see, we don't have to worry about what if when we have the what was." *Oh, that sounds good, said Atlantis. One of your better explanations.* They walked slowly, looking up and about, smelling the air, and kicking the leaves gently as they strolled. "I have something for you," she said as they meandered back. They could see the old veteran and Inja returning. "It's in my bag!" she exclaimed. "Put out your hand and close your eyes. I want you to guess, but no peeking!" she commanded.

Alabama did as told. "A rock?" he said after the object was placed in his hands.

"Yes, but not just any rock. It's my lucky rock. You can open now!"

It was indeed a rock, dull, grey, but out of the ordinary, nevertheless. "And lucky?"

"Very," she said.

"Well, if it's lucky, I think you should keep it," Alabama explained.

"No!" squealed Alice, "it's for you. Besides, you can't give it back; it's a gift."

"I will cherish it always," he said, blushing.

Alabama pushed the rock into his pocket. "I have something for you," he said. Then, retrieving it from his other pocket, he gave her the broken chip from the robot's head.

"Made in occupied United States," she read. She looked up curiously.

"It's so you'll remember me and the first days we met. If I had something better, I'd give it to you."

"No, this is great!" she exclaimed. "More than perfect, you see my gift is from where I was born, and this is from where you were born."

Alabama pulled the rock out and looked at it again. "Where were you born?" he asked.

Noooo, don't tell him, shouted Atlantis. He'll spoil everything! He won't mean to, but he will! He'll find out anyway; he already knows but doesn't know what he knows, Alice replied. You'll be sorry; you've already given him too much information! But Alice set Atlantis to the back and continued. "Luna," she replied. "It's a very rocky place."

"Oh, I've never heard of Luna, but I'm sure it is very nice if you're from there." The disbanding of the clouds was a reminder of the ending of the splendid day. There was little more to say. "May I kiss you?" he asked. "I'd feel kind of funny around the veteran."

"And Inja," Alice said. She laughed and then looked up into his face. "You know, I think we'll see each other again."

"I hope so," Alabama said and, leaning towards her, he whispered, "one kiss is barely enough to last a lifetime."

* * *

She knew what loggers could do; she had seen trees razed and cleared to make streets of asphalt. He knew frost on thistles walking along dirt paths on hot days. And like a vapor trail, the boy and the girl went in opposite directions. Such a thin breath, invisible to the eye, its billions of atoms ascend to the stars. The dog followed the veteran and the boy, and the girl followed the fairy rings. The old man and Alabama walked in silence with the dog on a lead because the veteran knew they would be approaching a place on the path where the dog shouldn't wander. And Alice found where the ivy crept on the broken walls and where the squirrels and birds build nests in piles of stone. There she waited for the sunbeams to part, and they led her to ten unmarked grey rocks.

Alabama stopped to watch the vultures circling overhead. Secrets eventually fall away as the wind picks up footprints in the dirt. The old soldier thought of the unburied limbs. They deserved no words. He motioned above, "it's a good omen; no one's going to bother you."

"Then, I can go home?" the boy asked.

"Yes, you can go home. We'll continue on to the hut and rest there for the night," he suggested. "I'm tired."

The silvery grey in the sky spoke for the boy's mood. To suffer without complaining seemed like a perfectly wasted sacrifice.

"I'm miserable," he finally admitted. He stopped abruptly and clenched the leash tightly in his hands. He turned to the old man.

"Son," the old man said, "if I had a tonic to ease your pain, I'd be a rich man. But I don't. I wish I could tell you not to feel sadness, but that would be a fool's errand. And if I said time would heal all, that would be a lie. So all I can do is say, the feeling you sense is an echo between you and Alice." Alabama thought for a moment. He was sure he could hear Alice say his name.

Chapter 27

The stones chalked in white were camouflaged by time. Tufts of dry grass feathered the spaces between each stone. Alice loitered around for a few minutes; nothing could be more certain, she had arrived. *Why the pale face? Atlantis asked. I'll be with you.* But the youth did not wish to spar with Atlantis and ignored the question. Alice never considered her accomplished task until the moment she caught sight of the sunbeams casting a web over the ground. The game of hide and seek was over. The solitary spot, which sunk deeper than roots, was shielded by ten stones. Alice walked carefully, orienting herself. It now became clear what "the mole" meant.

She recalled the day her father asked if she could keep a secret. He had reminded her about the canister and how the world would be different when she woke up. And then he said if she were to get lost to follow the mole. *What about the canister? Atlantis demanded. We don't need it, Alice said. It's in a good resting place, underground where father buried it. Don't you think it's kind of ironic, now you're going underground too, said Atlantis.*

The tenth stone was set aside, revealing four metal squares with steel rings. It seemed obvious what to do, but when the youth tugged on one of the rings, the square didn't budge. So she tried another and another. Again, none of the four squares moved. However, after inspecting the design, it became apparent that she did not have to pull at all but merely wiggle them apart effortlessly as one does a puzzle.

Light from below passed between the squares as she set them free. She kneeled at the edge of the opening, listening for sounds. She thought she heard voices laughing. *Atlantis, do you hear it? Right here in the earth, another secret. Will they remember us, Atlantis? Who, Alice?* The occupiers called them newcomers. But they were wayfarers, people of a lost time. They enacted a self-imposed exile into a zone defined by neither place or presence or geography, simply it is.

Some are told that life begins and ends with the earth. Alice looked up at the moon and lightly touched her neck. She thought of Doc and wondered if the woman knew they shared the same beginnings. She leaned over the entrance and felt her hand on the first rung of a ladder, and as if dipping into cold water, her entire body shivered.

* * *

In the defective landscape, where the fire had consumed the garden shed, the spirit of the youth emerged. No rain had fallen, yet released from the dry soil, sunflowers claimed the space. Inja pawed the ground, snorting the dirt from her nose.

Amazon, Danube, and Nebraska were the first to see, but it was Alabama who heard the flowers talking. These straw-colored blossoms, a gift rewarded by patience, interrupted the rhythm of their lives. For so long, days were reserved for Alice. Each had inherited a part of the stranger. They were the keepers of the sunflowers. They knew what they had to do; they would get jars, lots of jars. They would be ready for the first seed's harvest. So, bequeathed with a lilt of faith, they picked up the pieces of the afternoon and held them close.

Part VII

Alice's Detour

Chapter 28

She arrived at the yellow house camouflaged by wind-blown dust and the smokey glow of twilight. She knocked lightly and waited. "It's open." The youth entered and shut the door behind her. "I'm Alice," she said.

From across the room the woman gestured. "I'm Doc. Have you eaten? I have plenty." A candle was lit, its glow resonated warmth.

Alice walked towards the woman and smiled. "That would be very nice, thank you." The woman took Alice's bag and set it aside.

A tranquility of understanding filled the kitchen. A chance meeting or the reward of patience? "For the first time, I have no path to follow. I have legs but can't remember where they should take me. I don't know what I'm supposed to do," Alice said.

Doc nodded with empathy. "I understand, in fact, I know exactly what you are feeling. The test of time is a memory, but sometimes," Doc explained, "it's best to make your own."

The kitchen came alive, and the voices of Alice and Doc resonated through the open window. Such moments are rarely heard by others only to be shared by those inside. There was a renewal as if spring had finally arrived.

* * *

The youth was no longer the stranger.